Pirates 2.Arthemise De Lomvast

Luc Dragoni

Published by Luc Dragoni, 2024.

PIRATES 2.ARTHEMISE DE LOMVAST

First edition. February 28, 2024.

Copyright © 2024 Luc Dragoni.

ISBN: 979-8227908513

Written by Luc Dragoni.

LUC DRAGONI

Dear readers,
Thank you for your kind attention.
Your comments, your reviews, either laudatory or unfavorable, are always welcome!
LucD.auteur@hotmail.com

Chapter I – Ocean

Weariness

On the large, dark and varnished wooden desk, the red spider seems to be sleeping. A slight swell, peaceful and friendly, gently rocks the ship and the captain's cabin. Outside, the breeze is weak and many fogbanks surround the vessel. For the moment, on board, the only threat is boredom and the crew is dozing because the Topsail Schooner named 'Brigantine', although sailing under full sails, can hardly move. Indeed, the loch has just estimated a low speed of only three knots!

There is really nothing to do. The entire boat has been brushed and thoroughly cleaned, the sails and ropes have been checked and mended, only some repairs need to be done following the damages suffered by the last storm, and the cannons, still in perfect working condition, are ready to fire if necessary! Their shiny gray metal barrels appear through the ports left open, in case some merchant ship would come to sail in the vicinity. However, today like the previous days, these pirates have got nothing to get their teeth into...

"Cursed Mediterranean Sea"! She whispers, and then she begins to think it over...

Here the merchant ships do not carry wealth as sumptuous and imposing as in the new world. There are always the same goods: basic supplies, food, water, if what their barrels contain can be described as food and water! As for the wine, it certainly flows steady all day but it is most often acrid and pungent, just good enough for the throat of all these drunkards... the only one that would be rather good is directly shipped to the West Indies colonies, and Rum, this good old Rum extracted from our precious sugar canes, is particularly lacking in these areas and terribly expensive!

For her crew, she is not running short of food, this is quite the opposite, but since the beginning, in the company of all these men, she had become accustomed to offering and drinking some rations of this sweet beverage of the tropics. It had always put her heart into the work and made her happy!

Although she is still a very young woman, she remembers with a sense of disappointment these few friendly celebrations, and these good moments continually remind her of the time of her youth and her beginnings, often difficult, in this new pirate life. Indeed, it was a very hard time, but sometimes happy and also oblivious to danger! In spite of the drama she had been enduring, she lived an age during which she was always feeling fresh as a daisy, joyful and above all invincible.

But now she is bored, sad and upset. The few boardings they realized in this sea brought them only cumbersome goods, worthless, and difficult to store or negotiate.

In addition, all ships here carry similar cargoes: bundles of wool and cloth, barrels of wine or oil. Only silk, stuffs and spices are goals well worth launching an assault...

Obviously, this Mediterranean Sea is also an unsafe place for a pirate vessel as lonely as hers! Little unknown islands, always offering a welcoming and secret anchorage, are not frequent in these countries, and the royal armadas are moving everywhere. They parade arrogantly and exhibit their full power. As for the Barbary fleets, they usually possess several ships and her Topsail Schooner could not possibly fight against them, at best she would be able to escape!

The young woman cannot help but also think about this terrible disease, whose no one even dares to pronounce the name, but which can now be found on board some vessels and deep inside their cargo. This same atrocious epidemic that gradually manages to decimate an entire city...

"Mediterranean coasts!" She mutters to herself. "Impure and damned shores!"

On the Captain's desk, now her own desk, the young woman, whom everyone now calls 'Brigantine' like her vessel, immediately notices that the big red spider has slowly begun to move...

"You too my beautiful creature, you don't know exactly what to do and how to occupy your time... The fat insects that populate our tropical islands, those you hunt without any mercy, are few and far between in this part of the world! Where are our rainforests, lush vegetation and hot days, where is our soft and moist air?"

In a low voice, she speaks to her animal as if she were talking to a person and at times their eyes meet. So, nonchalantly, the young woman lays her emerald-green eyes upon the many little black eyes, definitely removed from any sensual expression, of her strange hairy companion. She has also put her long hand very close to the beast and is now tapping lightly on the wood of the table with her damaged fingertips. The spider seems to have understood what her supposed mistress wants, because little by little she cautiously climbs on the back of her hand and continues to climb up her arm, constantly and delicately feeling the skin and then the sleeve of her black garment, ending up clinging to her shoulder.

"That's good my beautiful one!" Whispers the Brigantine... "At least this time you haven't been afraid and you haven't thrown your hairs that cause so much pain, your hairs of misfortune! You know, you're now very lucky because you can walk around at your own convenience. When the 'Dragon' was still the captain of this ship, he didn't want to see you hanging around his desk and he was telling me all the time with his calm and deep voice: 'Listen, young lady, you keep your wild animal on you only, otherwise one day or another I'll soak it with rum and at last I'll burn it!'

The beast has just stopped moving, it seems amorphous and lifeless, with its long legs folded against its body. No doubt it wants to warm up because in these areas, even at the beginning of summer, this kind of creature might still be cold...

The young woman sighs while she thinks they would need a little skirmish. It could keep her crew busy again and give them a lot of fun harassing all these proud Captains and their stupid sailors, who in these so-called civilized places never managed to look beyond the tip of their noses or at best the end of their ships! She also wonders how she could have found herself so close to the kingdom of France, her native land, and yet feel like a foreigner...

It is true that she accepted the Dragon's last proposition. This savvy captain had momentarily preferred to hang up his weapons and be forgotten, by becoming the owner of a tavern and a distillery of rum. But he wasn't that old! For a few years, he had occasionally entrusted her with his Topsail Schooner, who was perfectly fitted for privateering, and with his crew, or rather their crew, as she had been living in their company for almost seven years. However, this time it was no longer a question of sailing in these warm seas and close to their favorite small islands. It was indeed a very long journey...

Moreover, the Dragon's ally and occasional accomplice, sometimes occupying the position of First Officer or Boatswain, the one who was called with respect and fear 'Master' or 'The Eye of Satan', had paid a good price to be repatriated in the company of three of his men to the great province located in the South of the French kingdom. Like the Captain, he had wanted to give up this life of wanderings and robberies, but as for him definitively, because he was no longer young and his health was more than often deteriorated. He even had to use a walking stick to move around. He probably hoped to find some employment on the spot as an adviser, counselor, negotiator or perhaps even as a tutor...

Thus, the voyage across the great ocean and the arrival in the vicinity of the imposing Phocaean city, whose everyone is now talking with fear, was the first long-distance navigation from the West Indies that the Brigantine had to carry out. During this last anchorage near the coasts of Provence she landed these four men, according to the orders she had received.

Of course, this exceptional Master helped her a lot during this first navigation because he is learned and skillful in everything, but for the return journey, although assisted by a crew entirely devoted to her cause, she will be alone, since from now on she is the new Captain of this magnificent Topsail Schooner, and she will not even have the support of a First Officer.

Since their arrival she had also decided to extend their stay in the Mediterranean Sea, in order to discover a world she did not even know and benefit from lootings she then imagined much more fruitful...

"Ah, I made such a mistake!" She suddenly says out loud.

"I'm not interested at all in this Mediterranean society, and the profits of our robberies are poor. So, it's over! Very soon the crew will be summoned and the decision to return to the West Indies will be put to the vote. However, there will be no doubt about the outcome of the meeting, because of course everyone will want to leave!"

And she carries on with her monologue, seething with rage:

"And to leave an lasting memory to these arrogant Mediterranean sailors, we will manage to sink a few more ships before escaping by the narrow passage of the Gibraltar rock..."

However, she knows that when they finally arrive at this place, with her crew she will have to proceed as she did on the first journey. Once again, they will have to use some wickedness and try to look like a peaceful merchant ship...

Again, she is talking to her spider:

"Yes, my beautiful hairy, I will lower your flag, the same flag that terrifies all these fools, and we will raise the flag of one of these mighty kingdoms. It will be easy because we have them all! It would just be necessary to raise the most suitable flag at the right time, in order to quietly cross paths with other ships that we could have previously well identified."

She goes on to speak to herself, as if she were giving her orders in the presence of the entire crew:

"For us, it won't be complicated: English vessel in sight, we raise the English flag. If it's a French ship, then we choose the French flag, and so on!"

This is how the Dragon, her former captain, had taught her that she should never overestimate her power, nor disregard the might of her opponents. In fact, he had often told her these same words:

"Do you see, young lady, the weapons of a good pirate are abundant and diversified. There are not only sword, pistol and dagger, there are also hiding, camouflage, escape, negotiation and many others that I will certainly teach you, but that you will soon discover by yourself."

Ah, this Captain she liked so much and she had sometimes considered as a guardian, or even maybe as a brother in arms, she now misses him so much! However, one day or another, young people must also become grown-ups and be worthy of the duties they are entrusted with.

At least that is what she was well determined to achieve, in order to go back to see the Dragon, and then be able to relate her travels and describe with pride her adventures and her battles...

One day, discovering that she had become independent and self-confident, he told her in a wise but firm tone:

"You have therefore reached the age of twenty-one, and from now on it is up to you to take final command of this crew and our ship. For the time being, I am withdrawing, and the Master, the Eye of Satan, will do just the same in the near future. But don't be afraid, all these men like you because they consider you as the child of this vessel and the daughter of the ocean. No doubt, when the election takes place, they will appoint you Captain unanimously. And if you agree, your new Boatswain will be our renowned 'Colossus', always wearing his red crest of hair on the top of his head! You know, he alone is worth twelve!"

Then he laughingly added:

"And from now on, your hairy monster will be allowed to wander on my desk as it likes, and so this place will be yours!"

The Brigantine closes her eyes and remembers these words and all these events. But how quickly time has passed! It has been more than seven years since these pirates picked her up and took her aboard their ship. However, nothing destined the very young Viscountess Arthemise de Lomvast to have an adventurous and seafaring life...

Arthemise, this first name that suited her so well, who are those who still pronounce it today? And yet this is the name that her parents had lovingly given her in homage to the goddess of wild nature and hunting, the powerful Artemis, because they were fond of Greek literature and particularly enthusiastic about the vast mythology of the Olympian Gods. And curiously, this name was to be perfectly appropriate for both the vigorous physics and the independent character of their daughter... But obviously this kind of thought was to be kept secret within a kingdom in which monotheism had been implanted since the dawn of time, as well as the Catholic religion, and especially since the revocation of the edict of Nantes!

The woman pirate lets herself go, she stretches her long legs on the edge of her desk and for a while she imagines herself becoming again the young girl she used to be, the bold and lively girl, the young girl to whom nothing bad could ever happen....

A new life

On this small island of the West Indies, the young Arthemise girl does not live according to the usual way of life for children of her age, who mostly stayed in their various homelands and whose sad and monotonous existence was slowly unfolding in the cold and belligerences of the French kingdom.

No, on the contrary, Arthemise seems to exist much more intensely within this warm and humid climate.

Always jovial and playful, she spends most of her days outside her parents' colonial home. The very young person, the wild and red-haired girl, enjoys wandering and strolling around without stopping. She often visits the slaves who work in the fields, she observes and admires with her wide green eyes the marvelous and luxuriant world that surrounds her... She has a lot of fun, she runs, she struggles, she doesn't learn that much, except for the occasional and brief teaching she receives from her parents, who most of the time keep particularly busy with their new business and the few slaves working in the plantations they have recently acquired.

Indeed, although they are part of the nobility, they can only employ very few servants, and it is also impossible for them to find a suitable tutor and above all to pay him correctly because they invested almost all their modest fortune in this exploitation. So, they preferred adventure to a more peaceful life that would have allowed them to stay quietly within the kingdom of France...

Arthemise was only twelve years old when her father, the Viscount of Lomvast, finally decided to invest a large part of his wealth in the acquisition of a sugar cane plantation on a small island recently conquered by the all-powerful Crown of France and located somewhere in the West Indies. The Viscount had served for some time in the Royal Navy, partly under the orders of the

'Count d'Estrées, Maréchal de France', and had therefore been able to carry out numerous explorations during his various campaigns in the new French colonies.

Then, the many acquaintances that the Viscount had at his disposal in the Great King Louis' court had enabled him to be allowed by his very gracious majesty to purchase a small concession in one of these New World settlements, with the assignment of making this land profitable and the duty of producing in abundance the resources that this place could provide.

Thus, on a beautiful day in April 1711, after lots of delays and difficulties in preparing the vessel, the small family eventually embarked aboard a magnificent Frigate named 'Le Havre De Grâce', in order to carry out this long voyage across the ocean, which would lead them to their new life.

Arthemise, the eldest of a sibling of three children, is already tall for her age and her constitution is robust compared to that of her brother and sister, so she is the only one who can accompany her parents on this adventure. The two other children, who were deemed much too weak to follow them on such a journey, had previously been entrusted to close relatives located in their home province.

However, the Brigantine doesn't truly remember that time, when they were still living on French territory, because over the years the alcohol aroma and the tobacco smokes partly erased her memory. She now only recalls her tropical island...

As for this voyage, which lasted about two months, the young woman has only unclear and confused recollections. She can merely remember the amazing things that had impressed her young imagination at that time, such as this stopover in the very strange 'Isle of the Dragon', as well as the violent storm that had beset them shortly before their arrival, and above all the sweet taste of this mixture of Rum and water that the Captain had finally served her at the end of the voyage. Also and perhaps unknowingly, the smell of the ocean, the beauty and the whiteness of the large sails, the incessant noises of the wooden frame, the masts and the ropes, the incredible height of the mizzen, main and fore tops, as well as the company of all these strong and craggy men will have permeated her for the rest of her life...

On board this ship, the young girl does not have any fear. She is not scared of this moving place that is totally unknown to her and if she sometimes shudders and turns around in the presence of some unknown object or strange event, it is only to return a bit later to the same place, because her insatiable curiosity always ends up prevailing.

As she is the eldest of their three children, the Viscount and his wife always seemed to have a slight preference for her. Of course, they would not like her more than the two others, it is not a question of love or tenderness, but realizing that she was strong, lively and constantly in excellent health, they had a less caring and protective attitude towards her than with the others. That is why they based all their hopes on her, so that one day she would probably manage to efficiently support them in their business, and why not end up replacing them, which at the time was not common, since the preferences were rather directed towards male descendants.

However, the young Arthemise is completely unaware of all these future projects to which she seems destined. His young age does not yet allow her to realize that his beloved father is a somewhat dreamy and idealist man, who has already decided that this famous birthright, whose community places at such a high value, naturally belongs to her even though she is a girl. And as if it were premonitory, the young Viscountess often behaves like a boy because she is sometimes independent, impetuous or even boisterous.

And yet, even though she is only twelve years old and cannot so early on be considered as perfectly feminine, her beauty and her charm are admired by all. She does not even know why men are so emphatically looking at her person, and especially at her eyes, whose green color is uncommonly pure. Moreover, she is not afraid to stare at them until one of them, embarrassed and clumsy, turns his face away. This has even become the girl's favorite amusement, who from time to time begins to peek at the people around her without ever lowering her eyes, until they look away. She always laughs about it because she considers these events as small victories!

On this great vessel, Arthemise moves wherever she wants to, she likes the company of these sailors who are always busy and sometimes rough. It doesn't frighten her the least! She feels comfortable dealing with these men because they are truthful and genuine, in comparison with the womankind who tends to annoy her with all its mannered habits, excessive make-ups and affected ways with sophisticated fan movements. In fact, from a very young age, she has always been particularly nasty to her governess, especially when it came to letting herself be patiently dressed and combed like a young girl of her rank.

But for her, this time is definitively over because this same sad and austere governess does not participate in the voyage, and the different maidservants who were always busy working around her and her young sister did not follow either. From now on, the only person who can still look after her is the Viscountess of Lomvast, her own mother, who shows little interest for appearances and prefers to dedicate herself to the good education of her daughter. Thus, every day, she tries to teach her some literature, the history of the French kingdom and the fundamentals of mathematics. From time to time, she also tries to tell her about the magnificent conquests and achievements of the absolute monarch.

Admittedly, the young child is gifted as well as intelligent, but she cannot stand still! Her mother's lessons never last very long because she cannot be completely satisfied by the lack of movement and by this confinement, even in a spacious and comfortable cabin.

Little by little, Arthemise is becoming a girl who enjoys wind and sails, ocean, waves and foam. She often likes to contemplate all these elements with her amazed eyes. Her long, almost brown, reddish hair always flutters in disorder along her shoulders, and her strands, which in the warm midday sun are becoming golden-brown and sometimes coppery, seem to follow the ship's movements at all times, and when the breeze gets stronger, they are like so many little flags whose dance can never stop...

The Viscount is a worried man who only cares about his settlement project and the future good business he thinks he will carry out in this colony. He does not take very much attention to his daughter. It seems that he has already given her all his confidence, and anyway, on board this ship, she can never go very far, and even less get lost. This middle-aged man spends most of his time studying the maps and drawings of his recent acquisition as well as the organization of work and production in this West Indies Island. But he is somewhat anxious. Even though he had already commanded domestic workers and military staff during his various campaigns, he does not know exactly how he would proceed with this new workforce, which is exclusively composed of slaves, whom he himself has never seen, and whose recruitment had been left to the former Intendant. After all, he sometimes thinks that he is just taking over an already-existing property with a well-trained farm staff, so it shouldn't be too much of a problem. Moreover, during a previous journey to the new world, he had been able to meet his future intendant on the spot and this middle-aged man had made a pretty good impression on him, since he had considered this man very serious, honest and hard at work, even though he sometimes showed himself to be authoritarian, angry and brutal towards those he had to command...

However, the Viscount appears somewhat disturbed by this famous regulation, this edict promulgated in 1685 by the absolute Monarch and in force in practically all the exploitations of these islands, this terrible 'Black Code'. Indeed, this man, who has often been described as a utopian, comes up for his time with quite humanist and even progressive ideas, which can sometimes appear to be scandalous, but which in his point of view could begin to emerge under his own roof. Thus, this Monsieur de Lomvast, who has already given preference to his daughter by placing his only boy in the foreground, has now decided to modify the black code in order to make it more flexible and somewhat bearable. Then he will immediately start to use it in his farm, because he considers that his workers will be more efficient if at the same time they are a little less miserable. As soon as they arrive at their destination, the Viscount intends to establish all this in detail, with the help of this hardworking and experienced man who seems to be his intendant...

The seven golden islands

The young Arthemise does not even have a vague idea of where this vessel is sailing, or the future life that awaits her. Her ingenuous mind hardly wonders about this long journey and the important changes that will occur in her new life. Certainly, her mother the Viscountess had briefly told her that the three of them were going to travel to a new place on the other side of the world which was still unknown to them, and they would probably not be able to see their French province again until much later, perhaps when she would have grown up and become an adult. But for a girl of that age and as carefree as she was, these explanations had remained confused. Indeed she wondered, but without much concern, what was precisely meant by the expressions 'at the other end of the world', 'much later', and also 'to become an adult'.

Thus, Arthemise is particularly interested in the present moment, without worrying about the past and even less about the future. The events that she is experiencing seem to suit her perfectly, because this voyage, which started more than twenty days ago, allows her to realize that the permanent cold and grayness that has accompanied them so far, have given way to an always bright sunshine and a distinctly warmer atmosphere. Indeed, the ship is now sailing along the coasts of Africa and all these new and a little strange landscapes that slowly pass under her eyes are not to displease the young girl, who by the way occupies most of her time wandering on the main deck and also on the forecastle and the quarterdeck of this sumptuous vessel.

On board, everyone is familiar with her and she is now almost part of the crew.

One day among many others, even though it was firmly forbidden, but true to her self-reliance and the vitality that characterizes her, she manages to escape everyone's attention and begins to climb, like an acrobat, on the rope ladder of the main mast, which allows her to reach the main top quite easily! Of course this is not the highest platform of the vessel, but once up there the young person always watch with attention and amusement the men who are still working on the deck and suddenly appear much smaller. His favorite game is to hail them and make fun of their astonished and worried looks!

Arthemise is also a stubborn girl...

For a long time, she has no doubt understood that she was the favorite child, who also became the only child on this voyage, and she does not fail to take advantage of this situation. However, although she never proves to be capricious, she does so at will. On that day, Arthemise decided not to come down from that promontory on which she feels so good, and this allows her to perceive just after the seaman in charge of the lookout, who has just announced it by shouting loudly, one of the islands belonging to the kingdom of Spain and located off the coast of Africa.

This ship, her crew and her passengers will make their last stop in this place, named pleasantly by the Viscount 'the seven golden islands', in order to prepare the great and ultimate crossing that will take them to the new world, a long journey which will keep them inexorably away from their kingdom and the neighboring lands on which they had hitherto spent their lives...

The duration of their stopover is short, barely a few days, the time necessary for a vessel of this size to carry out the essential supply of water and food, as well as the traditional gift exchange and some commercial activities.

From time to time the young Arthemise goes ashore accompanied by her parents and this new island climate makes her particularly happy. Here live few inhabitants, the port is rather small and the houses, in limited number, are all clustered near the coast. The young girl does not understand the language of these people, but she does notice that their way of speaking is warm, harmonious and sometimes singing. Nevertheless, their intonations can also be bitter and rough, appearing to come straight out of the deepest part of the throat. Sometimes some people also make short whistles while they are talking, which surprises her a lot! In any case, this island people always speak extremely fast, as if their subjects manage to pronounce three words while she and her parents could only say one!

Very often, the small family wanders not far from the village and the port, but on this land nothing is similar to what Arthemise used to see in her native province...

Here, the large, dark and humid forests, in which a rotten wood smell and an air of mystery always reign, are definitively missing.

Likewise, the fertile pasturelands that allow livestock to graze abundant and fresh grass, or cultivated fields whose colors always change, according to the seasons from bright yellow to dark green, do not exist in this area. As for the majestic castles scattered here and there in the different countrysides of the French kingdom, there is none in this place. On the contrary, on this island the landscape is very strange and sometimes even disturbing, especially at nightfall. Indeed, sometimes the hills are bare, bleak and covered only with reddish or black rocks, with strange and unusual shapes, sometimes one can see a uniform vegetation whose soft green contrasts with the dark red or bright yellow of some flowers. On the coast, deep coves hide small beaches covered with pebbles or thick sand, showing the same sad and monotonous color also corresponding to the surrounding hills and mounds, which do not fail to differentiate them sharply from the deep blue of the ocean.

Everything that can be discovered here has something to sharpen the young Arthemise's curiosity. However, even if she is brave enough, she can also experience a few moments of fright because she knows absolutely nothing about this world! When at the bend of a path she suddenly crosses the road of a lizard of such remarkable length that she cannot believe her eyes, and must decide to turn back, when, in wanting to touch some plants with astonishing and attractive shapes, or even to catch fruits with bright colors and which seem quite appetizing, she hurts herself painfully by pricking her fingers... But during her outings, what attracts and fascinates her the most is this large tree decorated with a top in the shape of a ball resembling a small bushy forest, whose scarlet red sap looks like blood. Moreover, while pointing to this majestic tree with an amused air, the inhabitants of this place do not fail to repeat to her these incomprehensible words: 'La Sangre del Dragon', and a sailor from their crew who had often travelled to these distant lands will end up translating this expression by 'The blood of the dragon'! Obviously, this new name is much appreciated by the young girl who, given her young age, had always kept many tales and legends alive in her imagination. Inevitably, from all that she has noticed here, and listening to the words of each other, she will not miss to call this island 'The Dragon Island'.

The Brigantine opens her eyes and begins to smile... She often remembered this anecdote about the 'Tree of the Dragon', and in anticipation of her definitive return to the new world, she gladly plans to make a stop in this mysterious island. The 'Isle of the Dragon', the first island she discovered in her youth, such an event cannot be forgotten...

And this strange place could well have become the secret lair of her beloved Captain, because he too had been nicknamed the Dragon! However, tired of her present existence, of this so boring moment, the Brigantine closes her eyes and joins her dream again, this impenetrable dream populated by her abundant memories...

The girl of the wind

The short stopover is ending, the crew has finished the vessel's preparations and very soon comes the day of setting sail. For this new sea-crossing, it will be the last departure, as until they arrive close to their new settlement, they will not see any land and the ship will not stop anymore.

Thus, the majestic Frigate begins to move under full sails, and the wind of the South Seas, well established but always friendly, pushes the vessel inexorably towards her final destination.

Arthemise resumes her onboard activities with the same ease and liveliness, as well as her usual endless mischief, but sometimes she likes to sit still on the forecastle, just behind the bowsprit. Her dazzled eyes contemplate the distant horizon and the triangular sails located right at the front, not far from the bow, which are filled under the effect of a steady and sustained wind, contributing to the ship's progress towards the other side of this wide ocean. The young girl is fascinated by this atmosphere and never ceases to look at the jibs and then at the sprit sail, the name of which she doesn't know yet, but which makes her smile because it looks like cheeks that we enjoy inflating before we blow as intensely as possible!

She then begins to discover that the ocean is vast and endless...

When the fog settles in, one can only look at a few cables lengths away, but when the air and the sky are clear, an extremely distant line appears, which describes a circle around the ship, giving the impression that the vessel is set in the middle of a huge navy blue plate.

While the last islands become invisible from the stern of the ship, the young girl gradually realizes that this vessel, the crew, her parents and herself had never been so far away from the rest of their familiar world. Until now and at regular intervals, she had been able to catch sight of coasts and shores but now, even when she climbs onto the main top, she can only see the infinite ocean. So, after only a few days, she finds this spectacle somewhat dull and becomes rather bored. Then, helped by some topmen, she learns how to make knots, and knots of all kinds. Some of them are really beautiful and some others are particularly worked. Her still small hands are agile and her young fingers easily slip between the loops. She also manages to remember their strange and magical names very well, which makes her experience a feeling of adventure and unknown, such as the grapple knot, the robber's knot, the hanging knot or even the diamond knot...

Arthemise also likes to observe what she considers to be big fishes, whose elongated mouth reminds her of a beak, and which sometimes seem to dance while jumping and diving around the ship in an incessant ballet of foam with a bright whiteness. She can also admire the many birds, which for some time follow the ship, probably in search of a little rest or a meager food, and then leave her as quickly as they arrived, to appear again the same day or a few days later.

Under these tropical latitudes, and in spite of a still winter season, the young passenger quickly notices that the length of days and nights are becoming almost equal. She is rather pleasantly surprised by this situation, because in her native province the winter nights were very long and cold, and the days were much too short!

When the weather is clear and the moon is already high in the sky, in the company of her mother, she enjoys admiring the beautiful sight of a very dark and frightening ocean that suddenly starts to shimmer and shine, as if in some places the water were becoming an endlessly moving and swinging mirror. In their cold and cloudy province, the small family rarely had the opportunity to contemplate a pure and starry sky, but from now on, even the Viscount, who often used to sail far away from the French kingdom, likes to join his wife and daughter, so that all three can benefit together from this silent, restful and poetic atmosphere.

From time to time, many sailors indulge themselves, not without mischief, to evoke in the presence of the young girl some stories as strange as frightening...

Indeed, some mornings, just after sunrise, sometimes appear on the lower parts of the hull, at the level of the planking as well as on the bow or stern, a few small grayish colored octopuses, which in places are brown. Seafarers are accustomed to this type of event, but many of them, who are rather superstitious, are convinced that the presence on board of this hideous and tentacular beast is always a bad omen for the rest of the journey. In addition, in the minds of several crewmen, it may also herald the imminent arrival of the famous giant octopus, which according to ancestral legends and popular beliefs would be able to swallow an entire ship at one time.

Without any doubt, no one knows exactly how some vessels could have suddenly disappeared... of course storms cannot explain everything!

Thus, these stories, which seem unbelievable to individuals imbued with wisdom and used to live on dry land, take on a whole new dimension in the middle of the ocean and greatly influence the minds of people on board. Even the most educated of them end up feeling helpless when they find themselves isolated from the usual world they know so well, because at that moment any event or observation, which would have remained minor or even unnoticed ashore, quickly becomes worrying within this immensity of the seas. And according to how things are stated, all those who take part in the journey can begin to believe in these legends, but of course without confessing their disarray to the small community.

Arthemise does not worry that much about the few small octopuses hanging on the sides of the ship, because apart from the color they are similar to the white octopuses that fishermen sometimes brought back from the vast bay located not far from the family castle in her native province. On the other hand, she slowly begins to admit that unknown and monstrous animals can sooner or later be discovered, but as her temperament always leads her towards curiosity rather than fright, she simply wonders if this giant octopus could be the size of a big dog, a horse or an entire ship...

However, the girl does not fear legends, on the contrary, she likes them! A short time ago, her youthful mind imagined that a Dragon might have flown around the 'seven golden islands', and now she can also think about that enormous octopus supposedly hidden beneath the ship, in unfathomable depths...

Undoubtedly, the new universe that she discovers little by little is populated with very strange creatures and this tends to fascinate her, like those silver fishes that suddenly come out of the water and start to fly in the same way as birds! In fact, some of them finish their crazy race by suddenly falling onto the deck of the vessel and then shaking their wings frantically, hoping to fly again, but unfortunately their short existence ends at this precise moment, because they are almost immediately knocked down by one of the sailors and carried towards the galley to be given to the cook. Therefore, Arthemise has sometimes the opportunity to taste this new dish but she always wonders if it is really a fish, because in the middle of the flesh she cannot find these tiny sharp fishbones, which usually come to painfully sting the bottom of the throat. On the contrary, she notices small bones that immediately remind her of those of insignificant birds. On the other hand, this food, once well prepared, looks like the fishes she had often eaten, but with a light chocolate taste, which makes the whole thing quite enigmatic. However, the best part of this strange animal is its eggs, and when this one is filled with them, the girl, first of all surprised by their greenish color, appreciates very much this fresh, slightly spicy and quite maritime taste, which makes her assume that it must be the true flavor of the great ocean...

Thus, all these events and stories are continually adding to what Arthemise had in mind when she was still living in the family estate. Indeed, she never hesitated to venture alone into the great forest adjoining their lands, which had once been the favorite hunting ground of the ancient kings for the wealth of its game. Although forbidden to do so, she liked to visit the old lady who was living totally isolated in the depth of forests, and whom the local population considered at best as a poor and mad woman and at worst as a witch practicing mysterious rituals and terrifying spells. Nevertheless, Arthemise did not fear her, and the woman of the woods, who cherished the young Viscountess, never failed to teach her some secret of former times and also talk to her at length about the wolves, her loneliness companions. However, despite their present considerably reduced number, they still used to scare the surrounding population, to such an extent that people who had to venture into this place generally preferred to be accompanied by big and ferocious dogs. Arthemise, for her part, was going there alone, as if nothing bad could ever happen to her. She learned a lot from listening to this so-called witch, because this one seemed to know almost everything about the mysterious great oaks or beeches with magical powers, the various weeds to be picked and becoming good medicines and the supposed treasures well hidden in the dark forest ponds.

Anyhow, during this voyage, this rather wild girl, nicknamed by her own father 'the girl of shade and forest', was slowly becoming on board this ship the girl of sun and wind...

South Seas

And the interminable voyage goes on, slowly but inexorably.

The carriage ride from the family castle to the large port, both military and merchant, from where they embarked to the new world had already taken too long, according to Arthemise opinion. This beautiful fortified city was however only about fifty leagues from their family domain and their displacement had barely lasted five days. So, on this ship, and despite all the observations and activities she can do, she is really starting to wonder why her parents decided to take her with them, and whether this last crossing, which has been going on for more than two weeks now, will end soon. In addition, this increasingly warm atmosphere sometimes makes her regret the sweet summers of her native province located in the northern part of the French kingdom, during which the days become particularly long but the heat is never unpleasant. In fact, this northern region is permanently bathed by fresh air from the inlet that separates it from the English kingdom. On the other hand, here in the middle of the ocean, the heat is intense, moist and often suffocating.

Arthemise realizes that her skin, which is not used to such a sunshine, sometimes becomes reddish and even begins to itch. Likewise, she often suffers from a very strong thirst, accompanied by some dizziness. She is always annoyed when these misadventures occur, because in this case she must stay out of danger for a while in the cabin her parents occupy on board the ship, but she usually prefers to rest on the lower deck because in this place the atmosphere is much more lively and entertaining. So, commonly, one or two days later she feels much better and can go up on the main deck again!

Nevertheless this afternoon, curiously, the brightness is not as aggressive as usual. Indeed, a veil of clouds very high up in the sky, some of which are rounded like small pebbles, masks the powerful sunlight. At the same time, the sky is gradually changing color from a crystalline blue to a slightly bluish gray, which does not fail to intrigue the Captain and his first Officer, posted at the top of the poop deck.

When the family was still living on their property in the north of France, the young Arthemise, who spent most of her time outside the castle, used to know very well the late summer thunderstorms, sometimes violent, that were bursting over the nearby forest or along the coast. However, she did not have any knowledge about those that prevailed in the tropics.

Always watchful but still very quiet the captain observes carefully, using his spyglass, the large cloud that has formed very slowly and is still quite far ahead of the vessel. He also looks at the horizon on port and starboard sides.

The young girl, who at that time is not far from him, manages to hear his words clearly:

"Given the wind direction, we will not be able to escape it! Let's get ready to cross it, but we should try to keep away from its central part."

She quickly understands that the Captain is talking about this huge cloudy mass, now quite visible, which is somewhat lying on the surface of the sea, just in front of the ship's prow. Its top is of an immaculate white and has rounded parts that seem to rise ever higher, without ever slowing down their ascent, and when the gaze goes down, this imposing mass becomes shapeless and gradually darkens to an almost black color as it reaches the waves. The thickness of this ensemble also tends to shrink in the middle to widen exaggeratedly at its base and at its top, which has an increasingly flattened shape that reminds Arthemise of the anvil of a blacksmith.

The sun has now completely disappeared, hidden forever by this cloudy monster.

The young girl, who until now had never seen a cloud so high or so massive, considers in her fascinated eyes that it is indeed a monster, filled with hate and ruthless...

Actually, as the ship gets closer, unless it is the cloud itself, she briefly notices a few rays of light both yellow and white, so clear, bright, and jerky that it temporarily forces her to lower her head and look only at the ship's deck. The flash of lightning that she sometimes had the opportunity to contemplate from the family castle, the surrounding fields or the nearby forest does not in any case look like the violent illumination of the sky that she is now contemplating.

As for these low rumbling sounds, which are becoming more and more audible and frequent, they make her imagine that this colossal monster, against whom they will sooner or later have to confront themselves, has gone into a fantastic and extravagant anger that nobody and nothing would be able to stop or at least calm down.

Although the sun has become invisible, the heat is now overwhelming, and the wind that has been regularly blowing from the northeast since the beginning of the journey has become variable and totally uncertain. The surface of the water has also completely changed in appearance, from a dark blue to a dull grey that is now more similar to the color of the cloud than the one of the ocean. A deep, sneaky swell, laden with scum of which white streaks are endlessly lengthening, also begin to appear, as if it had suddenly begun to fearfully and submissively obey the giant nimbus that dominates and constrains it. The Captain has already given his orders, and the first Officer and the Boatswain are commanding the topmen to quickly use the brails to gather almost all the sails up against their yards before they could be furled. Only some topgallants and royals will not be furled, and the driver sail will also be kept to help if necessary with the maneuver.

The ship, although she is an imposing Frigate, is beginning to be tossed in every direction as if it were a simple rowboat...

Now the huge cloud has ceased to appear in different parts that could be detailed and clearly separated from each other, it has become much more uniform. It has turned into an immense greyish mass that masks the horizon along its entire width, and when the impressed gaze succeeds in revealing it from top to bottom, it occupies the entire sky, and little by little, this grey color gives way to an ink black that seems sooner or later to become able to swallow up the bow of the ship. In the midst of this gloomy nimbus, a few clouds' fragments still appear floating at mid-height, but the vague dimness of their shapes proves to be rather derisory compared to such an unattractive background. Suddenly, a rather cool wind begins to blow and gust, and the vessel, who pitches and rolls more and more, forces her tall masts into an incessant and uncontrollable swinging movement from port to starboard and from front to back. All the men whose presence on deck is not absolutely necessary have been asked to go inside their cabins or down to the lower decks, and then all the hatches have been perfectly closed. On the main deck, only two or three sailors, among the strongest and most experienced, are remaining accompanied by their boatswain. As for the Captain, majestic and apparently invincible, he stills stands upright on the quarter deck with his best helmsman.

Against her will, Arthemise had to join her parents inside the cabin left at their disposal during this voyage, but not willing to miss anything of the spectacle of battle that is preparing against the elements, she does not fail to observe the outside through one of the port-lights precisely looking on the main deck.

Suddenly, the gusting and violent wind has ceased, but the swell still continues to toss the vessel and it gives the impression that the cloudy mass has just stopped its crazy run just above the ship, as if to tell her that the fight is finally about to begin.

Immediately the young girl notices that a first drop of water has crashed heavily onto the main deck, not far from their cabin door; and then a second drop falls down in turn and a third one and so on... These drops are voluminous, almost equal to the size of a small bird's egg, and they seem weighty because when they reach the wooden deck, they make a loud noise and then bounce to spread out by flooding the whole place. Very soon, it becomes impossible to count them, and from now on, the heavy rain is becoming like a continuous and impenetrable curtain. The rain is so intense that Arthemise can barely make out the dark trunk of the masts, but sometimes, through this veil of water, she can see the bow of the ship with her bowsprit that suddenly dives into an even higher wave. This wall of water then falls down strongly on the main deck, temporarily producing an impetuous flood of which foamed water mixes with rainwater, before draining powerfully away through the starboard and port scuppers.

The girl holds firmly the doorjambs because she absolutely wants to stay at the same place and contemplate these raging elements. So, what she has been able to observe for the first time is repeating itself at will!

In addition to the pitching that continually lowers and raises the prow, there is also the roll that tilts the ship so steeply that the top of her tall masts sometimes skims the white and foamy ridge of the highest waves, and then this endless list movement starts again but is directed to the opposite side.

This storm seems to never end, as if the entire world was suddenly drowned in an ocean of violence...

Until a short time ago, the afternoon was rather sunny but now all the brightness has disappeared and it seems that the night has finally fallen on the ship. Only powerful flashes of lightning that tear the cloud in all directions bring a brief, aggressive and blinding light. The thunder rumblings of this cloudy monster, which were heard some moments ago in the distance, have become deafening and they look more and more like brutal cannon fire.

Arthemise wonders if there is another place, if there is anything else that can be found close to this cloud. Is it big enough to cover all or part of the ocean? No one can know that. If the sun is shining in some other location, then how far away is this peaceful area?

When the vessel is pitching down or rolling to either side, the girl can glimpse the sea for a very short moment and the surface of the water seems to swell, as if it were momentarily attracted by this mighty cloud. This part of the ocean is also covered with a myriad of constantly renewed drops that rebound and split, continuously poured by the storm, like a gigantic waterfall.

The young girl cannot help but think about it, however, she does not dare to admit it... What a spectacle one must have from the main top! And of course, no one is ever allowed to get up there by such a storm.

The Brigantine also remembers this event and the thoughts she had at the time. Nonchalantly sitting in her captain's armchair, she begins to laugh. The main top, or rather all the tops and platforms, since the time when she was a young girl, of course she has come to know them... The mizzen top, the fore-top, and the highest one, the crow's nest!

She really enjoyed hanging herself above everything and everyone in any weather!

For this fearless woman, who has never been afraid of anything, or at least who has always been able to hide her fears and apprehensions, it was a game, a good way of taunting nature and showing her men that she could always surprise and overcome them.

But his laughter freezes because the long journey of his childhood belongs now to the past and the present moment is not to please her.

Then the Brigantine leans her head back, her long red hair swinging gently behind her back, and her tired mind lets herself be caught in this long sluggishness.

Chapter II – Tabago

New Granada

Behind the wooden door of the cabin, little by little Arthemise notices that the monstrous storm vomiting all its hate and retaliation begins to calm down. Lightnings are becoming more and more scarce and rumblings seem to move away. The air is getting colder and the sun, which had completely disappeared seems to offer again its brightness, but of course it is still shy and bleak. Severe rain showers also tend to decrease and give way to gentle, friendly and caressing rain. The girl observes all that with a careful eye and she is rather satisfied. This seemingly endless episode is almost over, but in the same moment, so subjugated by such a great outburst of violence, she is inclined to regret that it has already ended. The raw power of the raging elements exerted on her young mind a boundless admiration as well as an unlimited fascination...

Like all those who had taken shelter, Arthemise can now get out of the cabin she shares with her parents and return to the main deck, still copiously wet. The rain has now ceased, and although a certain swell is still maintaining, the hatches have been reopened because from now on, the Frigate will no longer be in any danger of being submerged by one of these massive rolling and breaking waves, or by the torrential streams of water that ran down from the sky just a moment ago and turned the deck into a mere reef washed and flooded by surf. The young girl watches the Captain, soaked from head to toe, but remaining undisturbed and cheerful. This episode didn't seem to have upset him that much and he doesn't fail to exclaim when he sees the Viscount who is approaching:

"It is quite normal, our route, further south than usual, brings us closer to the coasts of New Granada, and here in this season the rains become abundant. We should have left in January but the refurbishment and the fitting out of this vessel lasted much longer than expected. For sure, we will meet thunderstorms like this one again!"

But considering the serious and gloomy face of the Viscount, he adds:

"However, Monsieur le Vicomte, when we finally catch sight of the coast, it'll mean that we have nearly reached the West Indies, and at that time there will only be two days of journey left."

Arthemise climbs up with her father on the quarter deck and can't help but look at what remains of this cloud that has caused so much trouble. The sun has just reappeared and a steady and friendly wind pushes again the ship, which immediately runs under full sail in the required direction, finally heading southwest. It seems that the blackish monster who was thundering and grumbling unceasingly above them has gone away, calmed down, indifferent, no doubt to bring his anger to another place, unless he finishes his course somewhere else in the infinite sky.

During her last week of travel, the Frigate 'Le Havre De Grâce' will be forced to endure some more events like this one, but for a few days now the blue and pure water of the great ocean has gradually taken on a brown hue...

It seems that some sea currents originating from the many rivers of New Grenada are moving far away from the mainland to come and caress the sides of the ship. This turbid water drains a good part of the country's soil offshore, whose mud carried by thunderstorms and torrential downpours at the beginning of this wet season inexorably sweeps down the slopes of the hills, and then lets itself be taken away from the mouths of rivers.

The ship and her crew are slowly approaching these famous coasts of the new kingdom of Spain, but still without being able to see them, and more and more branches or foliages are drifting on the water's surface. Sometimes, the trunk of an unfortunate tree, undoubtedly removed violently from its original forest by some impetuous torrent filled with rainwater, comes to join and cross the route of the Frigate, which remains impassive, as nobody and nothing can stop her until the final destination.

The long and tedious journey finally seems to come to an end when one morning, shortly after sunrise, a coastline that the Captain apparently knows very well lets itself be discovered on port bow, and from now on the maritime zone on which the Frigate is sailing will appear as a wide area of muddy water, colored in brown or grey and sometimes in ocher or reddish.

Arthemise, still sitting on her small lookout platform, wonders whether the ship is sailing on the ocean or over huge moving plains of mud and sand. The spectacle that she can see reminds her of the river from her childhood, this beautiful river that was running not far from the family estate. When at last it was flowing into the sea, its mouth was still quite wide and sometimes also full of debris of all kinds. Today, however, this oversized river, of which she vaguely makes out the many meanders and ramifications, seems to have an infinite width and a considerable power compared to the one she used to know so well and which, once placed close by, would only look like a harmless and thin stream...

The Captain knows his job very well. During this long journey across the ocean, he always managed to steer his Frigate in the right direction. He is a bold and cunning man, as well as wise, because he chose to follow a slightly more southerly route, which certainly compelled him to cross a few big storms of the rainy season, but which also enabled him to reach first of all the vast continent, possession of the crown of Spain, and then slowly sail up the coast towards the small lonely island, the ultimate goal of this voyage, and located only two days away from their present position.

Thus, this first day in sight of the coast unfolds by slowly moving forward in the middle of the dull and brown waters of the mouth of this giant river of New Granada.

To enable everyone to finally discover the shores of this new world, the ship sails at just a few cable-lengths from the mainland. However, these places do not seem to be steady or welcoming, and no doubt it would be impossible to land directly on site, because the strong current generated by this river always tends to push the ship back offshore. The landscape then appears to be totally swampy and covered with bushy vegetation, mainly composed of plants and trees that seem to belong to both the terrestrial and maritime environment, with well-developed forested aerial elements showing a practically uninterrupted green mantle, and low parts with thick, unshaped and knotted roots looking like many large, rigid and immobilized ropes rising from the bottom.

The ship now follows a northern route, heading towards the eastern part of a rather massive first island, whose few hilltops gradually become visible, thanks to the ocher light of the golden sunset, but the coastline, hidden in the shadow of these hills, still remains mysterious. The majestic river, now located on port side aft, always evacuates its waters with power and contributes to the ship's progress by gently pushing her towards her final destination. Little by little the sea is leaving behind its brown color and is becoming tinted with bluish shades. However, under these latitudes close to the Equator, the sun goes down very quickly and a particularly dark night is immediately following, so that the water which surrounds the ship and which slides tirelessly along her sides to quietly move away behind her stern suddenly becomes black again, like when in the darkness they were still sailing in the middle of the great ocean..

Indeed, it is the last night that the young Arthemise and her parents spend on board this ship.

The Captain, a polite and friendly man throughout the voyage, has kept some provisions of wine and alcohol and is inviting the small family and the few officers in his large cabin for the last time, which occasionally has been used as a meeting place and a dining room. Fresh food, poultry and fruits have been exhausted for a long time, and unfortunately only salted pork, pulses and these awesome sea biscuits, as hard as pebbles, are all that is left to eat. But tonight, the precise last evening on board the Frigate, the many fishes caught this day will satisfy the appetite of the guests because the cook has been able to prepare them and liven them up, thanks to the aromatic herbs that he patiently preserved during the whole trip and whose he keeps the secret. Thus, by means of these delicious seafood products, this final meal shared in common is a constant reminder of this long voyage. Then, with the help of wine and alcohol, the atmosphere becomes perfectly relaxed and jovial. Unfortunately, on board the freshwater ended up getting a very bad taste, even though it had been kept in the best possible conditions, at the lowest and coolest place in the hold and by transferring the barrels as soon as they were consumed, so that they would always remain full. Therefore, and for some time now, this water had to be mixed with vinegar to remain drinkable without risking all kinds of diseases.

But tonight, this very bad drink will not be given to Arthemise because the Captain has decided to mix this water, of course not with the usual vinegar, but with this new alcohol made from the juice of sugar cane whose popularity and enthusiasm continue to grow amid the local populations but also among all those to whom it can be offered or sold.

Of course, this wise captain had made sure that a reserve of this excellent drink was always present on board and, moreover, this voyage will allow him, once again, to complete his cargo. Indeed, the island constituting the birthplace of this first-rate 'eau de vie' is situated not far from their current position, and farther north is also located this Dominican monastery, partly transformed into a distillery, which also produces this kind of admirable nectar.

"Well, 'Mademoiselle la Vicomtesse', what do you think of this drink? Does it make water more digestible?" asks the Captain to the young girl.

Although in everyday life, Arthemise behaves most often nearly like a wild child, she has got pretty good table manners, because rules of polite attitude and pleasant habits that were taught by her former governess and her parents have permeated her forever.

However, she likes to keep people waiting for her answer, and while all the guests watch her carefully, she takes the time to taste this flavored water, while staring at the Captain with her wide green eyes, which does not fail to somewhat embarrass this man...

She then quietly decides to answer:

"Yes sir, this drink is particularly sweet and pleasant, but what's its name and how is it prepared?"

"Well, British gentlemen call it a grog. This is a mixture made of three measures of water and one measure of this sugarcane alcohol called 'Rum'. Believe me, this name will quickly become famous all over the world, and it will last forever!"

"The blending you have just made is really delicious, thank you sir."

Arthemise still continues to enjoy what the Captain has served, but while the guests are discussing things, mainly about their long voyage, the new settlements of the French kingdom, the politics and wars waged with much bluster by the great King Louis, little by little and at this large table, the young girl begins to display an absent expression on her face. For her, the sound of voices and conversations looks more and more like an incomprehensible and disorderly tumult. The atmosphere of this evening was already quite warm and yet Arthemise feels an even more intense heat, an irresistible fever which insidiously applies itself to invade her. Her ideas have tended to become intertwined and confused, and never before had she known such a state of mind, but as she finishes her drink, she thinks this brand-new beverage is definitely excellent!

And now the young girl experiences a sensation of well-being that suddenly makes her feel very happy, and from time to time it causes her to laugh a bit. Of course she doesn't burst with laugher because she is aware that her maintenance in the presence of all these people must be dignified and blameless, but her appearance which was rather serious and indifferent at the beginning of this dinner has become imperceptibly smiling and cheerful. Arthemise examines the guests one after another to make sure that she still is in this room and in their company, but no one pays any more attention to her presence because from now on the conversations are well under way. How long has this meal been going on? She could not say it, as she has lost all sense of the present moment... At first she was bored because she thought it was going to last much too long, because usually she does not like to stay locked up and participate in such a party. She would have preferred to remain in the open air and why not, faithful to her habits, perched on top of some mast! However, in her present state of confusion, the elapsed time has become indefinite and she can no longer even realize if the night has just begun or if it is almost over.

A few moments later, the dinner finally ends and everyone slowly gets up from the table. Like this small group, Arthemise also stands up straight, but she immediately experiences a slight feeling of dizziness and it seems that her usually agile legs have suddenly become particularly heavy. The girl who commonly liked to walk in the lead, is just wisely following her parents to the main deck, keeping her eyes fixed on the ground so as not to risk stumbling. Indeed, the Captain as well as the Viscount and his wife, decided to go and appreciate the calm and freshness of this very last night which is just beginning.

It is certainly not tonight that the young girl will climb up to the main top!

Leaned on her elbows at the ship's rail, Arthemise just keeps watching the sea while the waves, lightly covered with foam, glide gently along the planking. She also contemplates the sky, as black as the ocean, because this is a night without any moon. However, all the way up there, a myriad of stars have begun to sparkle like diamonds and the tired but amazed eyes of the young girl slowly begin to make out them.

In her native province, the summer nights were never so dark and all these tiny luminous points did not stand out so well from the background of the vault of heaven, and if the observation was done from the windows of the family castle, the lights of the many candelabras greatly disturbed the perception of the beauty of a night sky. As for clouds and fog, they were frequent in that place and definitively prevented any representation of the stars. However, tonight, as the Captain's strong beverage helps to develop her imagination, Arthemise is truly overwhelmed by the spectacle she can admire, and her frame of mind, a kind of sweet sleepiness, now contributes to make this view even more unreal, immoderate and poetic. As the young girl lowers her eyes, she also discovers the flickering lights of the small wooden fires scattered throughout the large island that the ship is now following on its East side, and these faint uncertain lights are similar to as many stars that would be lying on the ocean surface.

Suddenly, Arthemise feels a deep fatigue, and a heavy drowsiness insidiously invades her. Her mother soon realizes it, because during this evening she constantly watched her daughter out of the corner of her eye and quickly understood that this grog had had a great effect on the very young person. Thus, the Viscountess passes her arm around the waist of Arthemise and takes her quietly to their cabin, in which the young girl immediately lies down and falls into a deep sleep, not without having several times swallowed her saliva in memory of this marvelous beverage whose so characteristic, sweet and flavored taste she will never forget again...

Turquoise

The dawn is rising and illuminates with its ocher and orange lights the small island which seems to be lying on the surface of the water, isolated but at the same time close to the big land spotted on the last day of this voyage.

The very long journey has just ended.

For this family of settlers whose new home will be located here, on the other side of the great ocean and at the very end of the West Indies, the French kingdom and this cold Northern Province, the birthplace of their lineage, are now becoming a vague recollection.

The magnificent Frigate 'Le Havre De Grâce' finally came to a standstill at anchor, located at a short distance from the island's only harbor, itself dominated by the small fort that was supposed to protect it, but which was nevertheless taken from the United Provinces by the Count of Estrée during one of his campaigns in the West Indies. However, this Marshal of France had been particularly lucky that day because the gunpowder magazine had unfortunately exploded and it was precisely located just below the room where the enemy command had settled!

This morning, the Viscount of Lomvast has get up very early for he wants to be present at the very last part of this voyage, and he does not fail to remember and laugh at this anecdote, which of course had considerably shortened the duration of the siege that the Royal Navy of the great King Louis was planning to carry out in front of this same island. And the Viscount, who at that time was a very young officer, is now back in this place, which had been occupied by so many different Kingdoms in turn...

This long-awaited day, just beginning, sees the rising sun illuminate with all its vitality the large bay in front of which the vessel has stopped her course, and from his position the Viscount can almost see the plantation and the farm buildings he acquired several months ago. The anchorage and landing place chosen by the Captain are the closest to the farm, and are also much more convenient than the entrance of the port, as they are less crowded to undertake transport activities both on land and at sea. A bit later the landing operations will be carried out using rowboats and this new existence of settlers in the West Indies will finally begin.

For the time being, everything is calm, both on land and on board the ship. The crew on watch during the night, and who perfectly managed to get the vessel to port, enjoys a well-deserved rest. As for those who have relieved them, they have neither the usual swiftness nor agility, because the end of this long journey in the midst of violent storms, and the excitement of the last evening, has left them more or less exhausted.

It must also be said that there is not much to do because all the sails have been brailed up and furled, and the two anchors are now firmly attached to some reef several dozen fathoms below the ship. In the near future, the necessary food and water supplies as well as the required caulking, sail repair and cleaning activities will also begin. However, the Frigate will not sail during two or three weeks, so all this work will be done gradually, day after day.

After a night in which her unusual and extravagant dreams were particularly frequent, Arthemise is finally opening her eyes but now she does not remember anything. Her forehead is wet with sweat and for the moment she just lies on her bed and watches the brightness of the dawn through a porthole of the cabin. She is alone, her parents are already up, they left the cabin earlier and on the Frigate's deck a certain excitement can be heard. The young girl immediately understands that they have arrived at their final destination because from now on the vessel seems immobile and just a light slapping comes to caress the hull from time to time.

"Come on, I must get up now, I shouldn't stay here." she says.

After having made some ablutions with the water that was remaining at the bottom of the small tub and briefly prepared herself, she finally appears on the main deck.

Some of the crew members are busy putting the rowboats to sea and the Captain and her parents are carefully looking after the manoeuver. It is therefore by this means that the two way trips between the vessel and the nearby coast will be carried out.

The Viscount, the Viscountess and Arthemise, accompanied by the Captain and a sailor in charge of the oars, take their place aboard the first boat after having gone down along the sides of the vessel by using a rope ladder, which has just been carefully checked for the occasion. In the second rowboat are four sailors and the trunks containing all the personal belongings of the small family, which will then be transported by cart to their future home.

During the following days, the crew will finally be able to dedicate himself to the tedious transportation of the various barrels to the shore, first in order to clean them and then load them into the carts provided by the people of the farm. A bit later, these casks will be taken to the nearest spring to be filled with fresh and pure water before bringing them back and storing them in the bottom of the ship's hold. These activities will be the same with fruits and all foodstuffs that must be added to the various subsistence products already on board the vessel.

For the first time, Arthemise, accompanied by her parents, sets foot on the sandy ground of the small island and she immediately notices they got out of the habit of walking on a steady ground. She is particularly surprised to see that the three of them tend to stagger and react as if they were always standing on the deck of a the vessel, constantly trying to keep a certain balance, which of course cannot be missing here. In spite of this temporary inconvenience, the young girl cannot help but admire the magnificent landscape that is offered to her amazed eyes.

The beach on which the group disembarked is very long, it spreads over the entire bay, from the small harbor located farther north near the small village, to the southern end comprising a rocky section that plunges directly into the ocean. The rest of this small headland is entirely wooded with vegetation showing every hue of green, but whose veritable height cannot be appreciated.

The sand is light yellow, almost white; the water is clear, transparent, but if you look a little farther away, the color of the sea is pale blue, slightly green.

The small island includes a range of hills with low elevation that stretches from north to south and thus represents its backbone.

Right in front of their landing point and located in the southwest, lies one of the plains that seems to be cultivable and fertile within this colony and it is precisely in this place that the small family will live from now on.

Bordering the beach and in the direction where the group will go to join the property, Arthemise can see the same trees she had already spotted in the 'seven golden islands'. They come in different heights, some of them have very thin trunks and others are leaning as if they were ready to fall. Most often, their foliage can be found only at the top, seemingly reaching the sky, or when these trees are low and stumpy, they come to touch the strand. Curiously, these leaves are all identical and also look like branches. They are long, very thin and sharp, with first a horizontal shape when they are still close to the trunk, but when they reach the tip they usually bend downwards. The shade created by this vegetation is not wide, it is really necessary to be placed very near the tree to enjoy it.

The young girl cannot help but compare this light shade, letting more or less pass the sunlight, to the dark and mysterious atmosphere of the great forest in which she loved to stroll. She is also particularly surprised by this thick and hard bark, which always seems to get out of the trunk by going upwards. At this moment, Arthemise thinks that it must be very easy to climb these trees, by using a bark thus placed to put down her feet, and then get upwards. This reminds her of the favorite position she used to occupy on the main top of the Frigate, whose tall mast she always admired and appreciated...

The girl is not at all familiar with such a warm and gentle sea. In her native province the coastline is inhospitable, unattractive, and the water is particularly cold. In fact, with her parents, she never dared to venture into places so dangerous in appearance. In any case and according to her knowledge, there are very few people who know how to move in the water properly!

Moreover, in the north of the French kingdom, the tides are powerful and extensive. Sometimes the sea withdraws very far away and a bit later the waves come back in a hurry and invade the coast again, then it is necessary to join quickly the shore if you do not want to be submerged and drowned. On top of that, in the large bay located near the family castle, the most disturbing places are those occupied by quicksand, which are not always found in the same areas. They can inexorably swallow a human being or even an animal the size of a horse, in a very short time if no one is close enough and able to rescue the unfortunate person by throwing a thick rope and trying to pull him out of that sinister zone as fast as possible.

On this point, the Captain has explained that in the vicinity of this island the tides also exist, like in any sea, but are very weak and remain almost unnoticed. As for the quicksand he had never been aware of their possible presence in these new lands.

In the past, during the summer and in order to refresh oneself, Arthemise sometimes used to walk on the foreshore, but never too far from the dry land, or close to the nearby river or even in the vicinity of the mysterious forest ponds. She happened to walk barefoot, knee-deep in water, and she often enjoyed gathering shellfish, catching fishes with her net, those which are unfortunate and trapped in a puddle and desperately waiting for the tide to return to sea, or even trying to grab the famous crawfishes with its powerful claws, of which taste is always delicious when broiled on the embers. However, for the moment, the young girl is especially attracted by this quiet, warm and welcoming sea, of which blue is similar to that of turquoise.

"One of these days, I'll have to learn to swim in this sea without risking to drown!" She says to herself...

Then, instead of looking inland and taking some interest in her new home, she prefers to keep her eyes focused on the splendid Frigate that brought them here. Now that she can see this vessel lying at anchor, just a few cables-lengths from the shore and waiting quietly in the middle of this great bay with blue waters, she notices that the ship is even more beautiful, majestic and powerful than when she could contemplate her from the deck.

Arthemise is of course happy to have finally landed on this island with a fragrance of paradise and she is eager to know this new existence that will begin very soon, but far from thinking about her cold native province, she seems to regret this magnificent vessel, so vast, so wonderful, with white sails and masts higher than the tall trees of her childhood forest.

Anyhow, this trip lasted a long time and everyone is satisfied to have finally arrived at destination, nevertheless, in the daring mind of the girl, only a short stopover followed by an exploration of the island would have been enough for her well-being.... Indeed, Arthemise thinks it would be much better to go back aboard the ship because from now on, although she has been bored from time to time, she considers that this ship represents both a refuge, a way of defending herself or fleeing if necessary, and above all a place that seems to avoid any constraint or supervision on behalf of the men, to belong only to the natural elements.

The young girl knows very well that unfortunately the Frigate will leave again, that sooner or later she will raise her huge sails and that this time she will not be part of the voyage. According to the orders he received, the Captain will take his vessel to the other colonies of the kingdom in order to bring letters, new Edicts and Charters, as well as weapons, ammunition, and anything else that might be useful to people living on such distant territories. He will also make sure to load the ship with the various goods that France is fond of and that are so valuable to its power and trade. At last, this experienced captain will leave the West Indies and will again steer the 'Havre de Grâce' through the vast ocean during the slow and peaceful journey back to her home port...

Gloom

"Good morning, Monsieur le Vicomte, Madame la Vicomtesse, good morning Captain. Did your voyage go well? We were getting worried, we've been expecting you for a few weeks now!"

Arthemise was watching the ship closely and she did not see the man approaching. His loud and hoarse voice abruptly put an end to her wonderful dream, her dream of sails, ocean and amazing tropical islands. She suddenly turns around and discovers this man standing a few steps away from their small group. She immediately stares at him but he does not pay attention to her presence, as if she did not exist, and it is particularly unpleasant for the young girl because she had always been used to receive a special consideration and to be treated with a certain amount of deference by naming her, like her parents, 'Mademoiselle la Vicomtesse' or at least 'Mademoiselle Arthemise De Lomvast'.

But who is this rude and boorish individual? she wonders...

At the family castle, the servants were always polite and they had also learned to speak in a low voice. Obviously, on board the ship it was not the same because of the sound of the wind and waves, most often the sailors had to shout to be heard. But here, on such a quiet and deserted beach, what's the point of this?

'We've been expecting you for a few weeks now!'

Why do we get such a reproach from the beginning? she thinks...

If what she imagines is true, they are in the presence of their intendant, and his work should consist in waiting for them without saying any word!

But the man is already hurrying to give abrupt and peremptory orders to those who accompany him:

"Come on, you lazy bunch, enough rest! Can't you see these trunks? So what are you waiting for? Unload them, bring them to the carts and take them to the Grand Case of the new master! Do I have to do it for you?"

For a short moment he stares at those he has just commanded with a terrible look and then he resumes:

"Forgive me, Monsieur le Vicomte, they are all the same, lazy bastards, good for nothing. As soon as we don't look at them, they stop working or they cheat, they pretend not to see what is to be done!"

Arthemise quickly realizes that her parents and even the Captain do not appreciate this way of going about things. They look embarrassed and do not know exactly what to say, then the Viscount finally decides to speak:

"Monsieur l'intendant Mordieux, there is no hurry, we have all day to unload! But tell me, how does it happen at the farm? Let's take a look at your latest installations, because since my previous visit, a lot of things have surely changed!"

"Monsieur le Vicomte, please get in my cart with your wife and you too, Captain, come with us. I'll show you around the property while these savages take care of the rest!"

Still not any word or a mere glance in the direction of the young girl who therefore begins to follow her parents, looking sad and gloomy. The Captain immediately understands her disarray and gives her a discreet wink accompanied by a smile.

Arthemise likes this man very much...

His authority is powerful and indisputable but above all quite natural, and his composure is exemplary. He does not need to shout to be obeyed, except of course in the middle of the storm, but in this case it is only for the purpose of being clearly heard and understood.

During the short way that leads them to the cart, the young girl takes advantage of it to detail the intendant Mordieux. This man is not very tall. It must be said that compared to her parents, who are rather tall and whose stature is slender and always elegant in any circumstances, the young Viscountess always tends to judge that their entourage is rather short. Her own mother is at least as tall as the intendant, and her father is nearly one head taller than this man, which certainly makes this individual look ridiculous, especially since his gait is irregular and swaying. No doubt it is the consequence of the shape of his lower limbs, which are a bit bowlegged. On top of that this man is not young either! He looks terribly worn out by a life that has already lasted too long, and his scruffy appearance is only matched by his wickedness and brutality. Of course Arthemise has immediately felt that this intendant must be particularly brutal, firstly by his manner of expressing himself, which is more like the barking of a dog than the words of a human being, and secondly because of what she has instantly noticed. Indeed, hanging from the belt of his dirty and faded trousers, there are two objects that tell a lot about this man's practices: a big stick and a whip. As for his shirt, it is as poorly groomed as his trousers and the whole is completed with a straw hat of the worst effect.

The group ends up going to the end of the beach and to the narrow dirt road on which the carts have been placed. Arthemise does not fail to observe the few Negroes who come down in the opposite direction towards the boats. The young girl is amazed to see them so closely because, apart from their stopover in the 'Seven Golden islands', she had never heard of such a population. But on these islands, that day was the very day of trading activities as well as the slave market, and although she had wanted to come closer to satisfy her perpetual curiosity, her parents immediately took her away on the pretext that this spectacle was certainly not meant to be viewed by the eyes of a young lady.

In addition, the presence of Negroes in his northern province had been always poorly reported. Indeed, with the many battles and skirmishes that had taken place during all these years, Arthemise had mainly learned to discover the faces and appearances of English and Dutch soldiers. Thus, the young girl examines these strong men, walking barefoot and only dressed in miserable pants, shirtless with brawny torso and skin as black as the darkest night when all the fires have been definitively put out. However, these Negroes walk with their heads down, they do not take their eyes off the sand, their looks are dull, sad and resigned. They move silently, in a silence of death, and Arthemise can only hear their breathing, slow and powerful, resembling a deep breath, coming from a natural and wild strength. The young girl, her parents and the Captain follow the intendant quietly and they are now only a few steps away from the cart that is to be used for them. At the front is an old horse with a brown coat and a completely white mane. The animal is quite dusty, it looks tired and impatient. From time to time, he punches the earthy soil of the small road with his heavy hoof as a sign of annoyance. No doubt he needs to return to the property to quench his thirst in his drinking trough.

"Damn slaves, they could at least brush it!" Grumbles the intendant.

Then the man invites the Viscountess and the Captain to take a seat in the back of the cart while he asks the Viscount to come and sit next to him on the bench at the front. He immediately gets on the cart and grabs the reins. With a violent kick he releases the brake that blocked one of the wheels and shakes the bridles. Then he suddenly shouts:

"Giddy up!"

The ground is still wet from the previous days' rains and the vehicle is struggling to move forward with cracking noises from all sides. The intendant unwinds his whip and in order to stimulate the horse, makes it crack first on the ground and then on the back of the animal, whose walking however does not become faster.

"Giddy up, old nag! Are you against me too? Hanging around like all those niggers?"

And the cart is moving not too well, limping along on this bad road. In some places the soil is dry, dusty and its brown color becomes lighter, almost grey, but in the ruts, where there are still a few puddles of water, the soil is transformed into mud and the cart already in poor condition has the greatest difficulties to move. The intendant is red with anger.

"That's how this damned horse will end up blocking our wheels in the clay! Giddy up, giddy up!"

And the whip cracks again.

"Let's see, Monsieur Mordieux, please stop this yelling! At worst, if we get stuck somewhere, well, it doesn't matter, we will go on foot. After so many days spent at sea, we will surely enjoy a short walk!"

Arthemise would like to get down and continue by walking along the roadside and close to this luxuriant vegetation, but the cart has not yet found itself completely immobilized, so she must stay quietly on this dirty and partly moldy bench. She then exchanges knowing glances with the Captain who says quietly:

"I feel sorry for this man. He seems constantly overwhelmed by events. If he were a member of my crew, he would have already been put to hard work, then placed at the bottom of the hold with bread and water until he learns good behavior!"

Despite the inconvenience caused by this encounter with their intendant, the girl and her mother cannot help but laugh. And the Captain carries on with his speech:

"I pity this poor horse! I hope that one of these days it will give him a good kick and knock him down!"

After having suffered the unpleasantness of this chaotic path to the end, the team and its passengers are finally getting out of what the locals call the savannah, and little by little the farm can be discovered as a whole. Some hedgerows separate the wild vegetation from the sugar cane fields, and within these plantations the harvest is already well under way. Indeed, in this season, it is necessary to have finished work not later than midday, and before the heavy rains occur, as they always make any outdoor activity very difficult to realize. The intendant stops the cart just after passing the last hedge and begins to describe the property:

"Here is your farm, Monsieur le Vicomte. As you can see, it's harvest season. Every morning, beginning at daybreak, I send these Negroes to slice the canes and during the afternoon we continue the work inside the farms buildings. Just in front of us, on the other side of the plantations and above this little hill, you can see the Grand Case. This will be your home. Right underneath are the slaves' cabins."

Without waiting any longer, the man shakes the reins and the cart starts again. From now on, inside the property, the road widens and finally becomes much better.

In spite of the distance separating them, Arthemise gazes at these sturdy and agile men, who never cease to cut the upper part of these plants to one or two feet off the soil, before stacking them on the ground and tying them up so as to transport them later to the sugar factory. She can also hear their songs with sad intonation and jerky rhythm. These dull but powerful songs may help to give them some energy, unless they make them even more melancholic by constantly reminding them of their country of origin...

"But why do these men sing?" Asks the young girl.

She is indeed very surprised because the farmers who used to work in the fields around the family castle were never singing.

"Don't misunderstand yourself young lady, what you hear there is only the song of homesickness and despair." Replies the Captain.

"We have reached the first farm buildings, Monsieur le Vicomte. Here is the sugar factory and the bagasse warehouse, next to the water mill. We're lucky! Not far from the property flows a river and water comes directly here through this pipe."

Then the intendant laughs, and with a mocking tone he adds:

"It's always better than a mill powered by hand or a horse mill! With all these stubborn animals and lazy niggers! But let's go on, we'll pass the draining room and the oven."

Thus the cart continues, moving forward painfully, but while passing in front of the bagasse warehouse, whose doors have been left wide open, the Viscount suddenly asks the intendant to stop his carriage immediately. Although the interior of the farm building is dark, he has just noticed something that seems to worry him.

"Monsieur le Vicomte, here are only crushed sugar canes that will later be used as fuel! Don't you want to continue towards your home?"

The intendant looks embarrassed and mysterious. However, without answering him, the Viscount De Lomvast has already got inside the warehouse and immediately goes to that nook where the daylight hardly penetrates, but which has immediately attracted his attention. And what he suddenly discovers in this place amazes and dismays him...

A black woman, only dressed in a colored fabric loosely tied around her waist, is standing here, partly hidden in the darkness. She is hung from a beam by means of a long rope firmly tied around the wrist of her left arm, thus permanently stretched upward. In her back, her right arm is tied to the ankle of her right leg, which for the occasion has been bent backwards at knee level. As for her left foot, which could at least serve as her last support point, it is forced to rest on a wooden spike planted in the ground right there. And the terribly bruised sole of her foot has no choice but to hurt itself tirelessly on this sharpened piece of wood.

The Viscount cannot believe his eyes!

Of course this gentleman took part in many wars and is quite battle hardened, as the reign of the great King had a particularly aggressive and intransigent policy. Indeed, during his career as an officer he had the opportunity to see seriously wounded soldiers, dead persons, but also to meet prisoners who had often been harshly questioned. Why then, is this kind of abuse taking place within this property, now his own estate, and which seems to be working more or less normally? But what exactly is going on here?

"Monsieur Mordieux, join me inside!" Asks the Viscount impatiently.

The intendant locks the brake of the cart and gets down promptly, followed by the Captain, who, having probably seen or understood what was going on inside the shed, expressly asked the ladies to stay put.

"Well, what does that mean, sir? Untie that person right now!"

The black woman has tilted her head to one side but her eyes are remaining closed. From time to time she moans faintly and her entire body trembles from top to bottom, in an involuntary movement caused by great suffering. Being obedient and without waiting, the intendant complies by releasing the ties of the captive woman who immediately collapses on the straw littering the ground.

The Captain is attending this sad spectacle without saying any word but imperceptibly he comes closer to the Viscount in order to support him with his presence.

"Oh Monsieur le Vicomte... All this is the work of this Negroe of Momba, the slave driver. Believe me, this one has really no pity for those of his race! You see, this woman is being accused of stealing rum from us, probably to sell it later to pirates or Indians. She'll have to acknowledge her crime, but she's only been here for a few moments and she hasn't confessed it yet!" Says the intendant.

"Order that this woman be transported without delay to her cabin and ensure that she will be washed, healed of her wounds and given something to drink. The rest of us will continue on foot, our home is not far away."

"Very Good Monsieur le Vicomte, as you want. But if this woman is a thief, with all due respect, you shouldn't release her."

"That's enough, Sir! Carry out your duty! I'll meet you and this Momba later on."

While the intendant hails a few slaves to take care of the captive, the small group slowly continues its way up, leaving the last two farm buildings on its right, and after having walked around the sugar cane fields from above, they finally arrive in sight of the Grand Case. Having witnessed the whole scene, the Captain, who cannot be so easily duped, tells the Viscount:

"I don't think that this woman has been standing there for just a short moment. Given her pitiful condition, I would say she had been tormented for about an hour or so.

The Viscount nods, looking upset:

"It is also my opinion, but we'll clarify all this very quickly."

The Viscountess and Arthemise have suspected that something serious and inappropriate had happened inside the bagasse warehouse, but they do not know the details of these events yet. They rely solely on the Viscount's wrathful attitude, whom they have never seen in such a state of unhappiness since leaving France...

Grand Case

The surroundings of the new family home are quite pleasant. Trees of all kinds and plants with large multicolored flowers provide shade, freshness and enjoyment A small stream, tributary of the nearby river that borders the property, supplies a fountain that is summarily constructed, and the little pond thus filled occasionally rejects its overflow into a narrow water canal that flows directly to the vicinity of the Negroes' cabins. On its path, this fresh and pure water will be used for irrigating the small gardens conceded to the slaves, so that they can partly ensure their subsistence, thanks to the products of this modest cultivation. The water then continues its way to the sugar cane fields and helps to irrigate them.

A maidservant, dressed in white and smiling happily, is standing not far from the fountain. As soon as she can see the newcomers, she walks towards them, and in a French language with accents coming from far away countries, she warmly welcomes them. This servant, who says her name is Khaaly, inquires with great courtesy about the long voyage made by her new masters. She does not fail to look at the young Arthemise and compliments her with a sincere and loving smile:

"Mademoiselle is very pretty, really handsome! She says, taking her hand...

She knows very well that in addition to the service and maintenance of the house, she will also have to look after the young girl, and that seems to give her great satisfaction.

Arthemise smiles in turn and regains her self-confidence. Indeed, the first moments spent on this island have not been very enjoyable, especially in the presence of this rude and bad-tempered intendant.

She therefore seems particularly satisfied with her new servant. She loves her wide smile with teeth so healthy and so white that she had never seen such before. The same goes for the sclera of Khaaly's eyes, as white as the immaculate snow of the girl's childhood winters, which creates a surprising light in the midst of the intense black of her skin.

The young Viscountess, who has always enjoyed observing and detailing the people who were in front of her, comes across one surprise after another. As they stand fairly close to each other, Arthemise notices that the back of the servant's hands is black, while her palms are almost as white as hers. As for her hair, which she can now see very closely, it is short, compact and curly. She would like to touch it because she has never seen anything like this previously. So, all this arouses her curiosity, and this rather amazed attitude also applies to the handmaid, who pays close attention to Arthemise as well.

This young servant must be eighteen years old and probably she has been recently taken from her home country to live and work on this island. Until now, she had never had to meet a person with such red hair and pale skin. But it is Arthemise's big green eyes that seem to surprise and astound her the most...

However, the somewhat impatient Viscount begins to question Khaaly:

"Good, very good, but do you know where the man named Momba is?"

"Yes sir, he's in the sugar cane field."

Suddenly, Khaaly stops smiling and her shining face becomes full of worry.

"If you see the intendant, tell him that I am also waiting for him."

Khaaly is lowering her head and then releases Arthemise's hand.

"Fine sir."

With an air of resignation, the maidservant goes down the path that leads from the Grand Case to the plantations.

In the meantime, the family, always accompanied by the Captain, takes a place under the shaded gallery, located just at the front of the main facade of the house.

"Some very special events seem to be happening here! What do you think, Captain?" Asks the Viscount.

"Monsieur De Lomvast, you have served in the Royal Navy for many years and your career has been brilliant. However, I think you know little about life in our colonies." The Captain hesitates a little bit because he would like to advise the Viscount but he would not want to offend him. Finally, he decides to continue:

"Dear Viscount, your ideas are noble and generous. Nevertheless, I believe that they won't be easy to put into practice, because you see, the facts and incidents we have just witnessed here are not particularly original. They are most often dictated by the application of this black code, or 'Code noir', governing life in our possessions of the new world and promulgated in the last century by our all-powerful Monarch. Yes, Monsieur De Lomvast, all this is only the common lot of daily life in the West Indies!"

"Yes of course Captain, I am perfectly aware of that, but we shouldn't exaggerate! The people in place seem to be taking advantage of the power entrusted to them. Why should we mistreat our workforce unnecessarily? Will it be more laborious or more efficient? Before tonight I will receive the intendant and his henchman. I will tell them some of my new black code regulations that I want to see scrupulously respected within my farm."

"Monsieur le Vicomte, I will stay on this island for about two weeks. Then, with my crew and my Frigate, I will have to sail to our other settlements, and later I will finally return to our country of France. You will remain alone with your wife, Madame La Vicomtesse, and your young daughter Arthemise. This intendant and his assistant, as rude and brutal as they could be, will be the only people who'll be able to help you and, if necessary, protect and defend your family in the event of a conflict with the slaves, or even worse with the Caribbean Indians, and also with the pirates, who will sooner or later be hanging around. The few guards stationed in the fort located close to the port will eventually be able to intervene, but with much delay. So, Monsieur De Lomvast, although you are the new owner of this farm, please remember to command these two men with subtlety and far-sightedness, and above all, please try to avoid attracting criticism from other settlers living nearby. You can believe me, despite your apparent isolation, in these islands located at the end of the world the news goes fast, even very fast!"

The Viscount, slightly frowning, observes the Captain carefully:

"Captain, you are a wise person and a very good adviser, but I never intended to abolish or modify the black code in depth. I just want to amend it as far as the physical abuse is concerned. So, the events I have just witnessed do not even seem to correspond to any article of this code. However, I am well aware of the current situation and I will comply with your valuable recommendations."

While the two gentlemen are talking while waiting for the Intendant and Momba to come, the Viscountess accompanied by Arthemise has gone into the house and begin to visit the site.

This is a rustic house, entirely built in wood, of which walls are covered with planks coated with red, and it gives to the whole a mahogany color of the most beautiful effect contrasting pleasantly with the surrounding vegetation.

On the same level as the outside gallery, there is a large hall that can be used as both a living space and reception area, and which is directly accessible through the main entrance of the house. It has three windows, two at the front and one at the back, which makes this room particularly bright. Opposite is located the storage room for goods and merchandises, communicating with the previous one through a wide passage in the middle of the partition. This small room has its own independent entrance also looking out onto the gallery, as well as a narrow window placed behind the house.

Apparently, the former owner had added an upper story to the mansion, which now includes two bedrooms that may be accessed by a wooden staircase located at the back of the large first floor room. The various openings are not glazed but are composed of wooden louvers more or less openwork, like the traditional Venetian blinds that allow you to watch without being seen. In addition, these shutters, even when closed, allow a certain amount of air to circulate at all times, which refreshes the house during high temperatures.

The decoration of the house is understated. As for the pieces of furniture, they are composed of a table in each room and a few upholstered chairs. These simple furniture items are rudimentary but functional, they are mainly made of local wood, except for the majestic sofa, which is placed in the main room and undoubtedly brought on site by the previous owner.

After having visited the first floor, the Viscountess and Arthemise are getting upstairs to discover the bedrooms and their furniture. The two rooms are briefly equipped: in each of them there is a pedestal table, a chair, a chest, a bed with straw and cotton mattress, and also an old and large wardrobe but only in the parents' bedroom.

For a colonial dwelling located on a small isolated island in the West Indies, the installation still seems quite comfortable.

Arthemise particularly appreciates the panoramic view from the window of her future bedroom. Indeed, the Grand Case, already possessing a second floor, is also occupying a dominant position at the top of a slightly rounded hill. Through her window facing southeast, the young girl can see an important part of the large bay in which the Frigate is anchored but also the charming small cove hidden on the other side of the rocky headland. Thus, thanks to this exceptional position benefiting from a certain height, Arthemise is able to observe the southern part of the island's shores and this reminds her of the marvelous sight she had of the surrounding countryside and woods from the highest windows of the family castle, or the contemplation of the great ocean from the main top when she was still living on board the frigate.

On the other side, the window of her parents' bedroom allows to embrace the whole property at a glance: the sugar cane fields, the various farm buildings and even the small portion of the path that leaves the savannah and which the group had taken when they were coming from the large bay. The Viscountess and her daughter can now see the few carts loaded with their trunks and their luggage that climb up to the Grand Case.

Very soon, following the instructions of Madame De Lomvast, who for the occasion is going down to the first floor, the young maidservant, helped by the porters, will be in charge of tidying up all these effects in the chests, sideboard and wardrobe.

Through the same window whose the Venetian blinds have been left open, Arthemise, now alone in her parents' bedroom, can see the servant Khaaly coming back from the plantations and the Negroes' cabins along the path, accompanied by the intendant, having his usual gloomy and sullen appearance, as well as the one who was previously named Momba, the slave driver. The latter brings up the rear and holds his head high. He keeps observing Khaaly, in a way that is both authoritarian and curious, something that does not fail to upset the young Viscountess. Indeed, Arthemise has already become attached to her servant because she greatly appreciated the hospitality and spontaneous affection this one expressed towards her.

In order not to miss anything about the conversation to come between her father and the two men, Arthemise has decided to go back downstairs. While everyone will be busy tidying up the various things and effects, she will be able to come and stay near the fountain and the pond, pretending to play with water, but listening carefully to their discussion.

Shortly after, from her position of watch, she notices both the carts' drivers, the intendant, Momba, as well as the maidservant, who, pleased to leave the company of these two men, immediately hurries into the house to help with the tidying, but in her rush does not even notice the presence of Arthemise, cleverly placed near the fountain. As the two men are approaching, Monsieur De Lomvast and the Captain, who were talking while sitting on one of the benches decorating the gallery, stand proudly upright, and the Viscount, a little tranquilized by the Captain's peaceful speech, decides to talk:

"Ah, gentlemen, I was waiting for you. How is the young lady?"

"Everything is fine, Monsieur le Vicomte, the thief is not bad at all! You see, these people are very good at faking pain or sorrow. Fortunately, Momba knows them particularly well and he always manages to outwit their tricks and make them confess the truth."

At present, Arthemise knows well the behavior of the intendant, which is characterized by roughness, hypocrisy and lies. She therefore focuses her attention on the Negro Momba, who is even more impressive than the slaves she met in the vicinity of the beach.

This man, though barefoot, is at least as tall as the Viscount. By way of clothing, he only wears grey pants, which are much too short for his height and therefore reveal particularly strong calves. His torso, shoulders and arms are so muscular that one might think that his black skin is made of a kind of armor. As for his wide and strong back, he is marked with several scars of varying length, a sign that he once had to be beaten and whipped, before finally becoming the one who mistreats the others. He does not carry any weapon, no dagger, no whip or wooden stick. Hanging from his belt is a carefully rolled up rope, one end of which has a noose and the other a rather thick knot. This famous Momba keeps his head high but he does not pay attention to anyone. From time to time, he simply takes a furtive look at the Viscount.

"Monsieur Mordieux, this evening, I will send you the new regulations written by me personally and which will be applied without delay within my farm. Whatever the reason, I don't want that kind of abuse to be inflicted here again. Be sure to explain all of this to your help. You can now leave and go about your own business. Very soon I will visit this woman and question her by myself."

The intendant nods while the Negroe Momba is remaining silent. But as soon as the meeting is over, the two men turn around and immediately walk away along the small footpath.

The young Viscountess, who has just heard everything in great detail, is quite satisfied and also proud of the attitude of her dear father. Previously, Arthemise had been somewhat disappointed by the Viscount's silent and rather unassuming behavior in the presence of the intendant, especially during the recent cart ride to the bagasse warehouse, but from that moment until this last conversation, Monsieur De Lomvast has finally managed to show that indeed he was the real master, and his reaction has delighted the girl.

"This is not this uneducated and disrespectful intendant who will lay down the law!" She says in a low voice.

Arthemise can now join her mother, Khaaly and the porters to attend the installation and various tidying activities, while her father and the Captain calmly resume their discussion.

"Monsieur le Vicomte, you have set the record straight and I think that these two men have both understood you perfectly. However, unlike the intendant said, I do not think that Momba is a slave driver."

"What do you mean, Captain?"

"Well, just like you, I have been travelling long enough to know that the famous slave drivers can be found mainly along the coasts of Africa and also in the 'Golden Islands' on which we stopped. Sometimes it is tribal chiefs who sell captives among their enemy prisoners, or even among some members of their own clans, when the latter are beginning to question the authority of the local master or patriarch. Sometimes they are clever and sly traders who have perfectly understood how the slave traffic is organized..."

"Indeed, that's what I thought at first when I saw this Negroe. If this man were a slave driver, then what would he do here in the West Indies? Captain, I agree with you. This Momba must be a mere henchman, a slave too, but much stronger than all the others and perfectly able to carry out the dirty work of the intendant, by means of getting some benefits."

"Yes, that's right Monsieur De Lomvast, and since I imagine that in your trunks you brought your pistols, I strongly suggest to carry them permanently and make sure that they are well loaded. Sometimes a simple gunshot fired in the air can help to quickly restore order, so that a situation does not get out of hand."

"Of course Captain, you are a man of good advice and I won't hesitate to comply with your recommendations!"

"Monsieur le Vicomte, you know how much I appreciate your company but the day is well underway and I must now return to my vessel to give clear and precise orders to my Second in command and my Officers. These gentlemen, who are nevertheless perfectly familiar with their work, will then be able to carry out the various ship maintenance tasks and the necessary loading activities to the best of their ability."

"Thank you for your support, Captain! Do not hesitate to come and visit us at any time you want. You know that here in our home, you will always be welcome."

The Captain gets up, and after having respectfully greeted the Vicomte, passes close to the entrance of the main hall and bows politely before the Viscountess, without forgetting to address a friendly look towards Arthemise. In return the young girl immediately shows her attachment to him with a wide smile.

The slaves

On this island of Tabago, the days are slipping away quietly and life slowly begins to get organized. The family is now comfortably settled in the Grand Case. The trunks have been emptied and the many effects have been put inside the chests and wardrobe.

The Servant Khaaly is particularly efficient and gives complete satisfaction. She seems to really appreciate her new masters, and moreover a great complicity is developing between her and Arthemise.

Yet everything seems to keep these two people apart...

First of all the age difference. In fact, the maidservant must be approximately eighteen years old when the young Viscountess is only twelve. Then the physical aspect that represents a striking contrast between the rather pale child with long reddish hair, the child from the north, from the cold and rain, and the young person coming from the very hot Africa, whose skin is black and hair frizzy. Then about the language. If Arthemise speaks a rather correct French, Khaaly knows only a few words, always the same ones, that she pronounces in an approximate way and with an accent coming from unknown lands, forgetting or modifying some consonants and even whole syllables. However, all this does not in any way discourage the young Viscountess, curious about any new encounter, and who is apparently very interested in this young person with a strange aspect and a weird way of speaking...

Arthemise has clearly realized that Khaaly would never become her governess, because this servant without any education would have absolutely nothing to teach her. These repetitive and wearisome tasks of teaching are thus assigned to Madame De Lomvast, and sometimes to the Viscount when he manages to get away from his various activities.

Nevertheless, Arthemise, who had never really appreciated the austere governess of the castle and the numerous maidservants, to the point of making herself more than often unpleasant and disobedient, truly loves the company of Khaaly. First of all, the latter would not be able to give her any order, but sometimes would simply provide minor recommendations, then, since the young servant is already native from tropical regions and has probably been living on this island for several years, she can teach Arthemise everything that cannot be found in books. These are the mysteries and dangers of the green savannah, its strange animals and insects, as well as its exuberant plants with wonderful multicolored flowers.

However, the maidservant Khaaly does not live with her masters. Around midday, as soon as she finishes her work at the Viscount's house, she goes down to the family cabin, begins to pick up some vegetables in the garden and prepare a simple meal for the whole household. She must also take care of her many siblings, because like other slave families, the children living in the Negroes' cabins are sometimes numerous, and parents cannot look after them because they are mainly employed in the rough work of the fields and the various tasks to be carried out inside the farm buildings. It is the same thing at night but Khaaly still has a little less work to do, because her parents, who at last have ended their hard day's work, can help her at home before finally remaining quiet and being able to rest.

These days, the Viscount has decided to visit the nearby cabin in which the young woman, accused of theft, lives alone. This tiny house is located fairly close to the sugar cane fields, at the bottom of the hill where the Negroes' huts were built.

To get there, you either have to go up the slope a few steps from the plantations or down the path that runs across the whole land conceded to the slaves. Coming from his new home, the Viscount naturally chooses this second route because it also allows him to discover the housing of his workforce.

The path is moderately muddy but in some places more or less steep. Regularly, during the rainy season, this narrow passage is transformed into a stream of water mixed with mud, but today the weather is very hot and the soil is rather dry. Following the wise advice of the Captain, Monsieur De Lomvast has loaded his pistols and has put them on his belt. He is not that afraid of finding himself in danger, for he is the one who gave the order to free and carry the captive back in her cabin, but sometimes people's reactions can be unpredictable and it is always better to get ready for any eventuality.

The Viscount is also suspicious about the intendant and what he might have said about the ill-treatment inflicted to the woman. Indeed, he has already unfairly accused his aide Momba of excessive cruelty, whereas this henchman was probably only obeying his orders, so he could have just as easily told everyone that the new owner of the property approved and even demanded that such acts be carried out against those who did not behave correctly or who violated the rules.

Monsieur De Lomvast is thinking a lot about all this as he passes through the small village that the slaves, coming from their native Africa, had been eager to build as soon as they arrived on this island.

The huts are small, barely more than twelve feet in length by six or eight feet in width and their structure is quite basic. While most often some of them have a kind of framework with walls built of tree trunks and a roof made of palm leaves or sugar cane branches, other cabins are even more modest and appear particularly unstable and not very sturdy. These last shacks are made from a combination of bamboo and small woods covered with mud or moist soil mixed with straw to ensure cohesion throughout the construction. For the roof, a simple but long enough branch acts as a central beam, and in order to be protected from the scorching sun, rain or insects, this mere ridge is covered with reeds. Finally, in order to protect these cabins from flooding, a few shallow trenches have been dug all around, and sometimes they also border the small parcels of surrounding land. Close to these houses, which certainly are miserable but nevertheless well adapted to this tropical environment, one can see enclosures with more or less wobbly palisades made up of intertwined branches, which allow some slaves to cultivate vegetables, raise a few poultry and sometimes even a pig.

At this time of day the place is almost unoccupied, as men, women and the oldest boys and girls have left to work in the fields. Inside or near the huts, only very young children and others, who are just a little older, are in charge of looking after the village. Slaves who are temporarily unable to work because they are wounded or suffer from one of these terrible fevers are also staying on site. As for the small number of old people who are still alive but too worn out to return to the sugar cane plantations or farm buildings, they have to maintain and repair the cabins, cultivate the small gardens and look after the animals in the backyard.

Thus, the Viscount has slowly walked through this village of slaves and has been able to find out on his own how are living those who work in his exploitation. He has not exchanged any words with the people he has met. Moreover, as he was approaching them, they were quickly going into their cabins or, if they were too far away, they shyly lowered their heads and did not dare to look at him...

He knows he is the absolute master and all this population of slaves fears him terribly, because according to the black code he has got the power of life and death over his subjects. In addition, he remains convinced that the intendant has made preparations for his arrival by repeating to the Negroes that they had to work hard, sweat and exhaust themselves without ever saying anything or even raising their eyes. He probably did not fail to warn them or threaten them on behalf of their future owner.

While he approaches the hut in which this young woman lives, Monsieur De Lomvast is still wondering about the attitude he should adopt. His state of mind is rather morose in relation with the way of thinking and behaving that prevails within his exploitation, and he himself, the noble soldier who had never had any doubts, suddenly starts to hesitate. Indeed, if he shows himself to be accommodating and ready to forgive, he will immediately be described as a weak person and in his back everyone will laugh at him. He will become the laughing stock of all, not only in this place, but also in the neighboring islands. On the contrary, if he displays coldness, hardness and insensitivity, he will betray his own sense of generosity and mercy.

The woman must have been informed of the arrival of the Viscount, as she stays upright at the entrance of her cabin. She is leaning against one of the branches that supports the whole of this modest house, but she stands only on one foot, because the other, roughly bandaged with a piece of cloth, is still badly wounded, and so she can only lay it on the ground from time to time and just at the level of the tips of her toes.

As soon as this woman can see the Viscount coming closer, she speaks to him using the same words used by her African companions, words that are still as incomprehensible as ever, but to which Monsieur De Lomvast is slowly becoming accustomed.

"Hello Sir."

The young person seems totally frightened because she has instantly noticed the two pistols placed on the Viscount's belt and moreover she does not take her eyes off them because she knows perfectly well what it could mean: an immediate execution without due process, since the master has the power of life and death over his slaves. Monsieur De Lomvast immediately understands why this woman is terrified and he wants to reassure her:

"No, no, don't be afraid. I have just come here to question you. But you can't stand up, so sit down!"

"Yes Sir."

Then he tries to talk to her as slowly and clearly as possible:

"You are being accused of stealing rum, what do you have to tell me about it?"

"Yes Sir. I steal. Sorry Sir."

The Viscount is surprised by such a quick confession. What others have not been able to find out by making her suffer, he alone manages to get it from the beginning by asking a unique question. He does not know what to think. Perhaps he has immediately inspired the confidence of this slave or on the contrary she fears that he would kill her. Nevertheless, this spontaneous confession suits the Viscount particularly well!

"How much rum did you steal and why?"

"Two flasks Sir, two, for the Indians, they give me food, I'm very poor. My man is dead. I'm very poor..."

The young woman has spoken very fast, to the point that she is out of breath.

"All right, all right, I get it. You've already been punished. Stay here and take care of yourself. I'll send my servant to help you. But don't do it again!"

"No, never, no, thank you, Sir."

Monsieur De Lomvast slowly returns to his home. He is anxious and absorbed in his own thoughts...

So, the intendant was right, this woman is a thief. She is the one who stole the bottles of rum. But why didn't she confess her larceny when she was partially hung from that beam? Perhaps she was thinking she would be sentenced to one of the punishments provided for by articles thirty-five or thirty-six of the black code, namely an afflictive penalty or death sentence, unless she would be whipped and then branded with a fleur de Lys....

The Viscount is the one who put an end to her sufferings and this clement attitude finally contributed to making him know the truth. Actually, commanding slaves seems to be quite difficult! Henceforth, Monsieur De Lomvast will let his intendant work, helped by his henchman Momba, and he will intervene only if it proves really necessary. But no doubt he will no longer need to do so, because he has already forbidden his intendant to inflict corporal punishment and he has also amended the black code with his new regulations.

However, following the Captain's recommendations, the Viscount did not change much. In reality, he simply replaced or deleted certain words and phrases present in some articles that he considered not very generous or particularly violent and cruel...

Chapter III – Rum

The Black Code

Within the property, the corrected parts of this edict now appear as follows, each one denoting a will and a character trait of the Viscount. Nevertheless, their reading seemed really long and boring to Madame De Lomvast, who had to go through them in order to give her feelings, as well as to the young Arthemise, who occasionally ventured to read some parts, but very quickly considered these writings to be particularly wearisome.

And Monsieur De Lomvast patiently explains all this to his wife, each time presenting the original text immediately followed by the revised text:

"I occasionally intend to employ my slaves, the most trustworthy and deserving, to deal with the sale of the products of our exploitation":

Article 18

('Let us forbid slaves to sell sugar cane for any reason and opportunity whatsoever, even with the permission of their masters, under penalty of whip against the slaves, 10 Livres Tournois against the master who has allowed it, and the same fine against the buyer.')

'Let us forbid slaves to sell sugar cane for any reason and opportunity whatsoever, except with the permission of their masters.'

"I do not want my slaves to be arbitrarily deprived of the goods and possessions that I could have entrusted to them":

Article 21

('Let us allow all our subjects who live on the islands to seize all the things they will find in possession of the slaves in order to be returned to their masters when they have neither money from them nor known marks, and if their dwelling is close to the place where their slaves were caught in the act. Otherwise they will be sent to the hospital for storage until the masters have been notified.')

'Let us not allow our subjects who live on the islands to seize all the things that they will find in possession of my slaves. The inhabitants of the islands will just have to come and tell me what they have noticed.'

"With the following articles, I would like to be a little more generous than the other settlers":

Article 22

('Each week, the masters will have to give their slaves, those who are ten years old and over, for their food, two and a half jars of manioc flour, measure of Paris, or three cassavas weighing at least two and a half pounds each, or equivalent things, with two pounds of salted beef or three pounds of fish, or other things in proportion, and for children, since being weaned and until the age of ten, half of the above-mentioned foodstuffs.')

'Each week, the masters will have to give their slaves, those who are eight years old and over, for their food, three jars of manioc flour, measure of Paris, or four cassavas weighing at least three pounds each, or equivalent things, with two and a half pounds of salted beef or three and a half pounds of fish, or other things in proportion, and for children, since being weaned and until the age of eight, half of the above-mentioned foodstuffs.'

Article 25

('Every year, the masters will have to provide each slave with two sets of cotton garments, or four Ells of cotton cloth, at the master's discretion').

'Every year, the masters will have to provide each slave with three sets of cotton garments, or five Ells of cotton cloth, at the master's discretion.'

"As a new master, I wish that a spirit of justice and clemency could be expressed through these new writings":

Article 33

('A slave who strikes his master, his mistress, his mistress's husband, or their children, with bruising or bloodshed, or who strikes them in the face, shall be punished with death.')

'A slave who strikes his master, his mistress, his mistress's husband, or their children, with bruising or bloodshed, or who strikes them in the face, shall be tried and punished with death if he is guilty.'

Article 34

('And regarding the excesses and unlawful acts that will be committed by slaves against free persons, we want them to be severely punished, even by death, if need be.')

'And regarding the excesses and unlawful acts that will be committed by slaves against free persons, we want them to be tried and severely punished, if need be.'

Article 35

('Robberies, even of horses, mares, mules, oxen or cows, which have been committed by slaves or emancipated slaves, shall be punished with afflictive penalties, even death, where needed in this particular case').

'Robberies, even of horses, mares, mules, oxen or cows, which have been committed by slaves or emancipated slaves, shall be punished with afflictive penalties, where needed in this particular case'.

Article 36

('Robberies of sheep, goats, pigs, poultry, sugar cane, peas, millet, manioc or other vegetables, which have been committed by slaves, shall be punished according to the quality of the theft, by judges who may, if appropriate, sentence them to be beaten with rods by the executor of high justice and branded with a Fleur de Lys').

'Robberies of sheep, goats, pigs, poultry, sugar cane, peas, millet, manioc or other vegetables, which have been committed by slaves, shall be punished according to the quality of the theft, by judges who may, if appropriate, sentence them to additional works, or afflictive penalties if need be'.

Article 42

('The Masters who believe that their slaves deserve to be chained and beaten with whips or ropes will be allowed to do so. However, let us forbid them either to torture slaves, or to mutilate their limbs, under penalty of confiscation of slaves and extraordinary sanctions to be carried out against the masters').

'The Masters who believe that their slaves deserve to be sentenced to additional works, or to be chained, will be allowed to do so. However, let us forbid them either to torture slaves, or to mutilate their limbs, under penalty of confiscation of slaves and extraordinary sanctions to be carried out against the masters.'

"I definitely do not want to separate myself from my slaves, even if they have committed offenses":

<u>Article 37</u>

('Masters, in the event of theft or other damage caused by their slaves, in addition to the corporal punishment of slaves, shall be required to repair the damage on their behalf, unless they prefer to abandon the slave to the one to whom the damage has been done. They shall be obliged to make a choice within three days from the day of the sentence, otherwise they shall be deprived of the slave.')

'Masters, in the event of theft or other damage caused by their slaves, in addition to the corporal punishment of slaves, shall be required to repair the damage on their behalf.'

"Finally, I am particularly concerned about my interests and I don't see any of them if I kill a man who has become uncontrollable and useless, but who can still make me some money":

<u>Article 38</u>

('A runaway slave who has been on the run for one month, from the day his master has reported him in court, shall have his ears cut off and shall be branded with a Fleur de Lys on his shoulder. If he reoffends within one month from the day of the first complaint, he shall have the back of the knee cut off, and he shall be branded with a Fleur de Lys on the other shoulder. The third time, he shall be punished with death.')

'A runaway slave who has been on the run for one month, from the day his master has reported him in court, shall be sentenced to additional works and shall be branded with a Fleur de Lys on his shoulder. If he reoffends within one month from the day of the first complaint, he shall be sentenced to other additional works and he shall be branded with a Fleur de Lys on the other shoulder. The third time, he shall be sold.'

Thus, Monsieur De Lomvast, thanks to this way of proceeding, will be in perfect agreement with his conscience and honesty. Moreover, he will show himself in the best light, he will adopt the beautiful role of an enlightened humanist, and he will undoubtedly be greatly appreciated by his workforce. However, Madame La Vicomtesse does not entirely share her husband's opinions and from time to time she does not fail to remind him of it:

"My dear husband, your ideas are noble, benevolent and generous, but you have nevertheless allowed yourselves to modify an edict of His Graceful Majesty our great King Louis. Indeed, the changes you have made are limited and of little importance, but they may well upset more than one! I only wish that the application of all these new regulations remains as rare as understated, and do not draw attention and animosity from our neighbors as well as the wrath of sovereign power..."

Then the Viscount has thought it right to display in view of everyone, no matter if people know how to read or not, the parts of his amended Code that he likes the most and that he wishes to highlight, especially the articles concerning the Catholic religion. Indeed, even if Monsieur De Lomvast, like his wife, has always been interested in the vast Greek mythology of the Gods of Olympus, to the point of naming their own daughter after a name similar to that of an ancient goddess, he considers that it is essential to scrupulously conform to the Christian faith, particularly since the small community that he is in charge of is located within these new colonies, far away from the kingdom of France:

<u>Article 2</u>

"All the slaves who live in our islands will be baptized and educated in the Catholic, Apostolic and Roman religion. Let us encourage the settlers, who have bought newly arrived Negroes, to inform the governors and intendants of the so-called islands within eight days at the latest, under penalty of an arbitrary fine, who then will give the necessary orders to have them educated and baptized in due time."

<u>Article 3</u>

"Let us forbid any public exercise of any religion different from the Catholic, Apostolic or Roman religion. Let us want offenders to be punished as rebels and people disobedient to our rules. Let us forbid all meetings for this purpose, which we declare to be illicit and seditious, subject to the same punishment, which shall be carried out even against the masters who have allowed it and shall suffer in behalf of their slaves."

<u>Article 4</u>

"No commander shall be appointed to the leadership of the Negroes, if he does not profess the Catholic, Apostolic and Roman religion, under penalty of confiscation of the slaves against the master who has appointed him and of arbitrary punishment against the commander who have accepted the above mentioned leadership".

Article 5

"Let us forbid our subjects practicing the Protestant religion to bring neither trouble nor interference to our other subjects, even their slaves, in the free exercise of the Catholic, Apostolic and Roman religion, under penalty of exemplary punishment."

Article 6

"Let us enjoin all our subjects, whatever their occupation and social status, to comply with the days of Sundays and feasts, which are observed by our subjects practicing the Catholic, Apostolic and Roman religion. Let us forbid them to work or to make their slaves work on the so-called days, from midnight until midnight, in farming the land, manufacture of sugar and all other activities, under penalty of fines and arbitrary punishment against the masters and confiscation of both sugar and slaves who will be surprised at work by our officers."

Article 7

"Likewise, let us forbid them to organize the slave market and any other merchandise trade on such days, under the same penalty of confiscation of the merchandises that then will be at the market and an arbitrary fine against the merchants."

Article 8

"Let us declare our subjects that are not practicing the Catholic, Apostolic and Roman religion unable to enter into any valid marriage in the future. Let us declare bastards the children who will be born in such circumstances, which we want to be known and recognized as open cohabitation."

Article 14

"The masters shall be required to have their baptized slaves buried in the Holy Land, that is, in cemeteries intended for that purpose. And to those who will die without baptism, they shall be buried at night in some field near the place where they have died."

Finally, by putting up these last articles at the entrance of the sugar factory and also in the gallery located in front of his own house, the Viscount De Lomvast made everyone aware of the slaves and freed men's rights, as well as the punishments and sentences incurred by masters who might be too inequitable, brutal or unscrupulous:

Article 26

"Slaves who will not be fed, dressed and supported by their masters, as already mentioned, may give notice of it to our Attorney General and put their statements in his hands, on which and even ex officio if the reports come from elsewhere, the masters will be prosecuted at his request and free of charge. That is what we want to be observed for the crimes and barbaric or inhuman treatments of the masters towards their slaves."

Article 27

"Slaves disabled by old age, sickness or any other reason, whether the disease is incurable or not, shall be fed and supported by their masters, and in the event of their abandonment, the so-called slaves shall be placed in hospital, to which the masters shall be ordered to pay six sols per day for the food and care of each slave."

Article 42

"When the masters believe that their slaves deserve to do additional work or even to be chained, they will be able to proceed in this way. Let us forbid them from giving them torture, or mutilation of their limbs, under penalty of confiscation of slaves and extraordinary sanctions to be carried out against the masters."

Article 43

"Let us enjoin our officers to prosecute the masters or commanders who have killed a slave who was within their power or under their leadership, and to punish the murder according to the atrocity of circumstances. If there is any reason for their forgiveness, let us allow our officers to release both the absolved masters and commanders, without any need to obtain letters of grace from us."

Article 47

"The husband, wife and their prepubescent children shall not be seized and sold separately if they are all within the power of one master. Let us declare null and void the separate seizures and sales that will be made of them. That is what we want to do with intentional transfers, under penalty against those who would make the transfers of confiscation of the person or persons whom they have kept, and who will then be awarded to the buyers, without any obligation for them to pay extra charges."

<u>Article 55</u>

"Twenty-year-old masters shall be able to free their slaves by any means, without being obliged to give a reason for their emancipation, nor requiring parental advice, even if they are under the age of twenty-five."

<u>Article 56</u>

"Slaves who have been made universal legatees by their masters, or appointed executors or guardians of their children, shall be considered and known as emancipated."

<u>Article 57</u>

"Let us declare their emancipation made in our islands, let us declare their birthplace in our islands, and let the freed slaves not need our letters of naturalization to enjoy the benefits of the natural subjects of our kingdom, lands and country of our obedience, even though they were born in foreign countries."

<u>Article 58</u>

"Let us order the emancipated slaves to show a special respect to their former masters, wives, widows and children, so that the offense they have made against them will be punished more severely than if it were made against another person. However, let us declare them to be free from all other useful charges, services and duties that their former masters would like to claim against them or their property and estates."

<u>Article 59</u>

"Let us grant the freed slaves the same rights, privileges and immunities enjoyed by freeborn people. We want the merit of acquired freedom to produce in them, both for their people and their property, the same effects as the happiness of natural freedom brings to our other subjects.

A discovery

Since then, the intendant and his henchman have been following these new orders and recommendations, but they have neither approved nor accepted them.

However, news travels fast, and in the small island, among the other settlers and also inside the tavern located at the port, discussions about this new owner, who freely authorizes himself to modify a royal edict, are running wild and do not reveal much sympathy towards the Viscount...

No doubt that the Intendant Mordieux also maintains this wrong frame of mind, characterized by hostility and suspicion, particularly when he meets other people, but of course, Monsieur De Lomvast, as a fairly pure, honest and even somewhat naive man, does not suspect anything and is absolutely unaware of all these slanders.

In accordance with the articles he displayed and anxious that his small community may live with respect for the Christian faith, the Viscount, although he is neither a bigot nor a regular churchgoer, has found an agreement with the few Franciscan monks established at the priory located not far from the village, so that they can say a mass every Sunday morning in the Grand Case, summarily arranged for the occasion in a place of worship. In this way, the new master hopes to create a certain harmony and a stronger union within the group whose he is responsible.

Of course, Monsieur De Lomvast did not fail to give generously many offerings to this monastic order, which also contributed to persuade and delight the priests to carry out this office, precisely because their function in these colonies of the new world consists in evangelizing all these populations of Negroes and also of more or less wild and abandoned Indians.

As for the Viscount, he is particularly pleased that he does not have to move all the people of his community to the priory, but on the contrary that it is a priest, accompanied by monks or novices, who comes to his house every Sunday in order to carry out some confessions, and then to say the High Mass.

Arthemise is really disappointed, as when she landed on this island, located on the far side of the world, she was hoping to finally get rid of all these chores associated with religious practice!

Every Sunday, during the long voyage on board the majestic Frigate 'Le Havre de Grâce' who brought them to this remote place, the religious service was celebrated by the chaplain embarked for the occasion, but this short ceremony was more like a mere blessing than a real mass, and nevertheless the young girl was already feeling that it was a waste of time! Then, with a High Mass celebrated by Franciscan monks, these 'Lord's days' are likely to become as long and boring as those spent with more or less sincere due respect for religious traditions, when they were still living in the family castle!

Arthemise would prefer to wander far away, in the heart of this luxuriant countryside that surrounds the property, or still in company of her good and amazing servant Khaaly, to walk along the wide bay where they landed for the first time. She would also like to get to the bottom of the mysterious little cove located farther south, and inside of which it is possible to go directly from the Grand Case by taking the bad, narrow and craggy path that leads down to this strange and secret place...

Nevertheless, the Viscount and the Viscountess have decided differently, so that the young girl and the maid must attend the Mass.

During the religious service Arthemise and her parents stand at the back of the large main hall and Khaaly stays just in front of her masters. As for the intendant, when he does not pretend to have an essential and urgent task to perform outside, he finds himself standing on one of the side of the room, not far from the window and in the middle of the audience. Obviously, the Negro Momba is always with him, which has more or less a tendency to irritate Monsieur De Lomvast, but for the moment he is not yet looking to separate these two men.

Throughout this seemingly endless period, Arthemise spends her time gazing at the audience. She frankly has the impression that the slaves do not know exactly where they are or why they are staying here, thus gathered, every Sunday morning. Nonetheless, they are all present and remain silent and well disciplined.

However, the young Viscountess focuses her attention mainly on the monks, who officiates in this improvised church. She is particularly intrigued by the appearance of these so called God's servants. In fact, they do not in any way look like the ecclesiastics and churchmen she used to meet within their French province. These individuals are craggy, they have dark complexions, their faces are rugged with heavy and prominent features and their looks are imperious. They have large and calloused hands, a sign that they probably have to produce everything what they need on their own, cultivate the land or fishing. While some of these monks express themselves rather correctly, others talk the language of the first settlers of the new world, already heard during the stopover in the 'Seven Golden Islands', the same and quite fast way of speaking, and whose words and letters seem to roll like stones when they hurtle down a slope. Some of these men have also created a kind of combination between their own dialect and the French or English language, which makes the whole thing a bit absurd, totally incomprehensible, and does not fail to amuse Arthemise.

According to the comments of the intendant, who does not seem to appreciate them that much, these men of God usually buy rum and let it age in the cellar of their mission for their personal use, but also in order to sell it at a higher price to the few sailors passing through.

The intendant even suggests that these monks would occasionally carry out this type of trade with pirates. However, it is also the same type of business that the former owner of the farm used to perform, without failing to include the Caribbean Indians within his few customers. And the intendant to warn the new landlord:

"Very soon, once your installation is completed, all this beautiful people will come to visit your farm and try to engage in trade with you, Monsieur le Vicomte. You will learn to know them one after another: pirates, smugglers, Indians and so on..."

"Well, Monsieur Mordieux, you seem to have already met these individuals and I hope you will be able to give me some valuable advices, and then we will see what we can exactly sell them."

However, at the request of the French kingdom, the colonies of the West Indies had above all to produce mainly sugar, and it was for this reason that his majesty the Great King Louis decided to annex these distant lands and grant concessions to some of his subjects.

Each landowner must therefore comply with what is requested to manufacture. Brandies and rum are only produced to avoid wasting molasses, simple sugar residues, or less often when they are obtained directly from the distillation of sugar cane juices, in order to be resold at a higher price, and also to improve the quality of life on site, but in the latter case, sugar production may suffer and rapidly decrease! Nonetheless, thanks to this marvelous beverage, the settlers can also protect themselves against all kinds of diseases, they can make their life better and sometime increase their income significantly. These are the reasons why they all produce it in greater or lesser quantities and often illegally...

Sometimes on this island, monotony and boredom seem to sets in permanently. However, this kind of weariness does not necessarily exist for everyone. Arthemise is much too young to share her parents' worries, even though she occasionally notices their concerns, nor is she really aware of the sufferings sustained by slaves, although she is conscious of their particularly hard work and precarious or miserable living conditions.

The young Viscountess is especially enjoying the warm and attractive atmosphere of this so typical new world that she did not even know. Thus, some evenings, when her servant Khaaly has finished her work, and also on Sundays, as soon as the High Mass and midday meal are over, Arthemise likes to discover everything that the young slave can show her. Moreover, the few brothers and sisters of Khaaly often accompany them and it is always up to the one who, during these short outings, will be able to surprise or impress this new mistress whom they really appreciate so much.

These Negroes' children are quite carefree and have not yet really understood what their status of slaves would be like in the future. So, since Arthemise never exhibits an attitude of arrogance when she is in their company, they almost end up considering her as a friend, as curious and resourceful as their small group.

While Khaaly knows very well that she is only a slave, her activity as a servant in the Grand Case remains one of the least unpleasant tasks among all those carried out within this exploitation. Moreover, since she must also take care of Arthemise and look after her, it allows her to maintain a special relationship with the daughter of the Viscount.

Precisely, these days, the little group has decided to initiate the young Viscountess into something quite unusual and particularly surprising...

In a rather remote part of the savannah, a location that Arthemise never visited before, the small troop led by Khaaly has finally decided to stop. The place is dark and rather quiet, despite a few rare bird songs that can be heard coming from the treetops. There is a smell of moss and damp wood, the soil is soft and slightly spongy, but the intense heat is muggy and unbearable.

Khaaly has given her wooden stick to her oldest brother, who is barely eight years old and seemed to be waiting for it, and then she tells him:

"Come on, Toko, it's up to you now, do it like I showed you, Mademoiselle is looking at you!"

Like her companions, Arthemise has now become accustomed to the surrounding darkness and her eyes are finally able to distinguish on the ground, just in front of Toko, a small hole dug in the earth resembling a kind of burrow but much narrower than the usual fox or rabbit burrows that she was used to seeing during her walks in the countryside or in the forest near the family castle.

"But what kind of little animal may be hiding here? And why did we walk such a long time to finally discover only a miserable rat or a beast of minor importance?" She asks herself...

However, Toko has already begun to gently tap the stick in front of the burrow's entrance, while little by little he pushes its flexible end inside. Khaaly has immediately come to the other side and she stays crouched, waiting, her hands on both sides of the small opening.

Arthemise is really wondering at what kind of weird game her companions might play, and just as she is about to tell them that this place is worthless and they should go for a walk somewhere else, she can see some long hairy legs that first of all catch the wooden stick and then suddenly release it by moving backwards.

Khaaly is looking at her mistress with a smile:

"It's here, we must wait for it Mademoiselle!"

And finally, she adds to the attention of her younger brother:

"Do it again, that's not enough, again!"

Then Toko repeats the same operation. Tirelessly, he tries to lure the beast out of the hole by showing it the end of the stick and removing this one immediately, in order to make it believe that the wooden stick is an enemy or a prey. In view of the long hairy legs that she has already observed, Arthemise realizes that inside this burrow must be hiding some kind of big insect and this really begins to make her curious.

And then, suddenly, Toko's ploy begins to work and the beast finally comes out of its hole, firmly grabbed onto the branch he had handed to it.

What a surprise and what a fright!

The young Viscountess did not expect to discover such a big spider. She did not even suppose that such a monster could exist. She can't help but startle while taking a step back.

In the family castle, spiders were certainly numerous and were spinning their webs in various places. Arthemise used to see them often, even in her own bedroom and sometimes above her bed, so she did not fear them. But here, in this dark and isolated place, the presence of such a beast, bigger than a hand, is really surprising and also frightening.

Khaaly has quickly noticed the emotion and mistrust of her young mistress, so she immediately tries to reassure her:

"No Mademoiselle, it's not dangerous, it has already eaten, it's not hungry at all, it just wants to sleep, that's all! Now look!"

With a slow and precise movement, she grasps the spider by the middle of the body while her young brother gently removes the stick from its grip. She then holds it up in the air for a short moment, the time needed for the beast to calm down and stop moving its long hairy legs. That is when she decides to delicately place the big spider on her tunic at the level of her belly and soon after, the animal, who no longer knows where it is, starts to climb lazily, to reach first the shoulder, then the neck and finally the top of Khaaly's frizzy hair. Immediately, the young servant wears a broad and victorious smile towards her mistress.

"Your turn, Mademoiselle, oh no, don't be afraid, it's not aggressive! Take it slowly, don't be scared!"

Arthemise doesn't really know what kind of attitude she should adopt. She has always been bold and alert during her various walks in the company of Khaaly but now she does not feel comfortable at all. A terrible embarrassment is overwhelming her. If she refuses, if she does nothing or worse, if she suddenly leaves, she will later be ashamed of herself for the lack of courage she has demonstrated. Of course she will always remain Khaaly's mistress but the latter will no longer be her friend, just her servant and nothing more....

Then, in front of this small group whose cheerful faces watch her closely, she finally decides to imitate her servant and with a brief sign makes her understand that she has to lower her head slightly. So, Arthemise slowly moves on until she finds herself very close to Khaaly and the hideous monster covering her hair. The maid continues to encourage her:

"Well, Mademoiselle, it's not hostile, take it easy!"

The young Viscountess holds out her pale hand towards the blackish back of the spider which remains motionless, as if it were sleeping. She tries to imitate the slow and meticulous gesture that her servant made a moment ago by spreading her right hand fingers, but her wide-open hand, which is now only a few inches from the beast, suddenly begins to shudder...

"Don't tremble, Mademoiselle, come on, it's not nasty!"

The fair-skinned girl, who in the ambient darkness looks even paler than usual, has finally grasped the body of the big spider and is standing there as if she were paralyzed, while the creature has once again delicately moved its long legs.

"No Mademoiselle, don't squeeze it too tight, if it gets hurt, then it'll be aggressive, very aggressive! Put it on your dress and let it move around."

Arthemise carefully lifts up the hairy beast, and although she is petrified because she has never experienced such a frightening moment in her entire existence, she perceives a strange sensation of life in the palm of her hand.

Moreover, due to the contact of her fingers with the spider's hairs, the young girl sometimes feels some slight stings and sometimes a certain feeling of softness.

Never before had she experienced such an episode! But already, following Khaaly's advice, she delicately puts the spider on her dress, and after a short time the beast begins to go down, by moving first on the whitish linen fabric, then on the bottom of her leg and on her foot, which it covers almost entirely with its shaggy body, to finish its run on the ground by moving quickly towards its burrow in which it enters very rapidly in order to remain hidden again.

Khaaly, imitated by her brothers and sisters, is immediately smiling, and the whiteness of her teeth suddenly seems to brighten up this particularly dark place in the undergrowth. She then exclaims enthusiastically:

"Well done Mademoiselle! All right, you've not been afraid, you're very brave! Congratulations! But be careful, if this kind of spider is standing on her hind limbs or if it seems to blow, then for sure it'll bite, and there will be a lot of pain, a great pain! And it can also shoot a mist of barbed hairs straight into your eye, it stings and it really hurts!

"Yes Khaaly, thank you, we should leave it alone now, let's go home."

The little troop is finally returning to the Grand Case. Arthemise slowly recovers from her emotions and gradually regains her natural ease. However, she has just experienced an extraordinary moment and her thoughts are baffled and confused. Although she had been deeply frightened, she managed to hold this repugnant beast in her hand, and for a short time, she even felt that this strange contact could be somewhat pleasant. Moreover, she demonstrated her courage to Khaaly and to all those half-wild and almost naked children gathered for the occasion, who were watching her with a doubtful and amused eye. But anyway, what a moment of surprise and anxiety!

On the cheek of the Brigantine a tear is slowly running down...

But no, she says to herself, the Brigantine never cries because the Brigantine has got a heart of stone and a steely-eyed gaze! At least this is the image and reputation she had managed to build over the years.

And yet, she remembers the events that occurred that afternoon as if they happened yesterday! And Khaaly's words, which are still echoing in her head: 'Well done Mademoiselle! All right, you've not been afraid, you're very brave! Congratulations!

And quietly she rehearses in a low voice:

"All right, you've not been afraid, you're very brave! Congratulations!"

"My sweet and friendly Khaaly where are you now? And my dear parents, where did you go? But why did this tragedy had to happen? We were happy and carefree. Even this endless waiting time on Sunday morning, this long and boring Mass, how I regret it now! Anyway, for the time being, waiting, that's all I can do, and especially since we arrived in that sea!"

But the Brigantine does not like to cry. A single tear is enough, and immediately she feels humiliated by such a vulnerability. Then, inevitably and as always, it will make her even colder, more evil or cruel and without any compassion for her victims.

"You'll see, bunch of fools, you can believe me, the next boarding will be bloody!" She says to herself...

"And you, my beautiful hairy creature, you'll very soon be satisfied!"

As if she was trying to comfort herself, the young woman has just put her hand delicately on the back of the red spider, which sleeps peacefully on her shoulder.

Then, through one of the large portholes of her comfortable cabin, her tearful, but still intense gaze is drawn to the many, low and nonchalant clouds that are hovering above these endlessly calm waves...

The Pirates

For the young Viscountess living in this new world, the days are slipping away quietly, and the various activities, more or less interesting or maybe boring, are being repeated over and over again. But from time to time, some evenings, in order to break away from the monotony, accompanied by her beloved servant Khaaly, and although the latter does not particularly appreciate this walk, Arthemise likes to take the narrow and tortuous path, which from the back of the Grand Case leads directly to this small, secret and isolated cove, located in the southern part of the island.

Strangely enough, Khaaly does not like to visit this mysterious place. She has always known how to be fearless in the remotest and darkest parts of the savannah, places populated by strange plants and frightening or hostile beasts, but whenever the two young people finally reach the strand of this tiny bay, the servant Khaaly appears anxious and embarrassed. Arthemise, despite her young age, notices it very well. Moreover, during one of these walks, she cannot help but question her maid:

"What's going on, Khaaly? Tell me, what are you worried about? What's your fear?"

"Bad place Mademoiselle, we shouldn't come here, never, there is danger, great danger!"

"But at last, look! There's really no reason to be frightened by some fine sand and a few gentle wavelets!"

"No, no, Mademoiselle, this is not because of the beach, it's very pretty! But often here come strong and evil men, pirates, Mademoiselle!"

"Pirates? What pirates, Khaaly?"

"Always the same, with his crew, for the Rum Mademoiselle! The Captain seems to be a good person, he's quiet and polite, but his men are just bullies and louts! They're scary and have given me some concern, especially since Mademoiselle arrived on the island!"

"You're probably right, Khaaly, so let's go!"

"You will see them at the Grand Case Mademoiselle, when they come to meet your father. Sooner or later, maybe. But there's no danger up there, you won't risk anything!"

In this small colony, time seems to pass more slowly than in France, because despite the ongoing work of farming, this hot and humid climate sometimes turns the inhabitants into nonchalant and apathetic beings. Nevertheless, several weeks have already passed. The splendid Frigate 'Le Havre de Grâce', commanded by her brilliant captain, has cast off for a few days now, and is undoubtedly sailing peacefully to other French settlements located in the West Indies.

So, at present, the small De Lomvast family finds itself really alone, isolated from the rest of the world and in particular from their native environment, which was situated within provincial nobility when they were still living in the protection of the French kingdom.

From now on, the Captain's frequent courtesy visits have obviously ceased and the Viscount, his wife and Arthemise realize how unknown and sometimes hostile this new colonial world seems to be.

As the Captain had announced, the ones and only links that could still bring them closer to the society to which they were accustomed are the more or less appreciated presence of this intendant, as well as the Sunday visits of some Franciscan monks coming from the nearby priory. However, these servants of God are not very talkative and their way of speaking, made up of a vague combination of French and Spanish languages, is mostly incomprehensible. As for this Mister Mordieux, the actual relationship with this person is limited to the few essential conversations and commands necessary for the proper management of the farm. Moreover, indifference and mistrust are in order.

At the end of this morning among so many others, the sun is shining bright, but at this moment of the day the intense heat begins to be felt and the environment becomes more and more moist, oppressive, and even suffocating. Many clouds with puffy and fluffy appearance have already appeared and throughout the day their dimensions will continue to increase inexorably. These imposing and immaculate masses with their dazzling whiteness will sooner or later turn into a series of dark and threatening nimbus whose blue-black color will announce some new torrential rain. Tirelessly in this season, these same events happen every day, but it does not prevent Khaaly from cleaning the small fountain located just in front of the entrance of the Grand Case and whose evacuation is regularly clogged, due to the accumulation of leaves and twigs rushed towards the ground by these famous, violent and successive thunderstorms.

The young Viscountess stands idly by her side, because for the moment, as usual, she does not have any particular activity to realize, so she likes to spend some time with her beloved servant, whom she watches with an indifferent expression, and this is the case most of the time.

The great Negro Momba is also on site. He has been asked to take care of the spacious garden next to the master's dwelling, a task that he performs very well because he is familiar with all the plants that grow there and knows how to look after them and make them more beautiful. This work is one of the least unpleasant among the various activities of the farm, thus he has agreed with the intendant so that from time to time he may be away from the sugar cane fields or the various farm buildings and devote himself to the maintenance of this garden in place of any slave who, according to him, would not be able to handle it properly. In addition and during a few moments, this allows Momba to find himself not far from Khaaly, although she does not particularly appreciate the company of this rude, stupid and brutal man.

However, this morning, despite appearances, the young Viscountess and the two slaves are not the only ones to occupy the place, since other people are very close, occasional visitors, those who know, as they choose, how to be noisy or silent...

No one saw them or heard them coming up and yet they are really here. They have climbed up the path that winds between the secret cove and the Grand Case and now they appear, advancing slowly towards the fountain. Khaaly has just perceived a muffled sound and she is the first one to look up and notice them. She then whispers immediately:

"Mademoiselle, look! The pirates!"

Arthemise suddenly turns around while Momba, who also noticed their presence and suspected a threat of danger, gets close to Khaaly and her mistress. The young Viscountess carefully watches the three men who are now only twenty paces away. Never before had she had the opportunity to meet such individuals...

An animal with a tabby coat and which looks like a big cat, but that she cannot well make out for the moment, is lying on the shoulder of the one who seems to be the head of this small group. This man is of average height but his stature is massive. He wears a beautiful, creamy white linen shirt, fitted with a piece of leather on each shoulder, as well as a black wide-brimmed hat. His thick pants, also entirely black, are on top of superb leather boots of the same color.

The one who walks just in front of him is small but sturdy and vigorous, his torso is bare, his muscles are prominent and give an impression of strength, his skin is reddish, even copper-colored, and seems to be partially burned by the sun. A loosely tied piece of fabric covers his forehead and one side of his face. Undoubtedly, he has been severely wounded to the eye because even at a distance, the cloth, probably white at first but used as a bandage, appears intensely tinged with red. And

Finally, in the back, follows a kind of giant, much taller than the Negroe Momba, and whose partially shaved head wears a red crest of hair, a bit like a fighting rooster or some Indians of the new world. He is a tall man, close to the toise, and well positioned on his shoulder he holds an axe of impressive dimensions.

The pirates have quietly approached the fountain and their chief, who already seems to know the place well enough, first looks at Arthemise and then at Khaaly. Then he addresses himself to the two young people:

"Good morning Mademoiselle De Lomvast, Hello Khaaly, what a hot day isn't it? A little bit of rain would be welcome!"

"Hello sir, yes sir." says the servant immediately.

"Sir..." replies quite simply the young Viscountess, surprised that this strange man could already know her name, and she does not fail to cast an interrogating glance at Khaaly who immediately tries to explain to her in a low voice:

"I will tell you later, Mademoiselle!"

"Well!" resumes the pirate. "I can see that Monsieur le Vicomte has not yet come back from his plantations. Never mind, may we wait for him here?"

"Yes sir, you may wait here, he'll be back very soon, sir."

"Thanks Khaaly, now you can get back to work."

The chief intimates to his two men to stay close to the gallery that surrounds the mansion, while he himself quietly comes and goes not far from the fountain.

The pirate with the bandaged forehead seems very irritated by his wound, which must make him suffer horribly and forces him from time to time to move his head in a violent and brief movement, as if to get rid of something annoying and uncomfortable. However, at the same time, this little red-faced guy constantly stares at the Negro Momba with his remaining eye and in a particularly aggressive way, as if he was permanently trying to provoke a fight. However, Momba, embarrassed and undoubtedly frightened by the apparent savagery of this little man, looks away and acts as if nothing was happening.

"Midget!" exclaims the pirates' chief in a tone that suddenly becomes peremptory.

"Will you stop this stupid game right now? We did not come here to provoke a skirmish but to negotiate, to trade with the new owner of this farm, Monsieur le Vicomte De Lomvast. Then you can watch wherever you want, but let Momba work in peace!"

The pirate with the wounded eye seems to fear his master and immediately puts an end to this useless bravado that he initiated earlier against the slave.

As for the big man carrying the axe, he is standing next to one of the wooden pillars of the gallery and remains silent, motionless, impassive. His dark and severe but elusive look is not focused on anything in particular, he is indifferent to the world around him and remains quiet and insensitive. If suddenly he was asked to destroy the Grand Case and slaughter all the people working on the plantation, he would surely do so, with good blows of his heavy axe, with violence, coldness, and without any remorse.

Now that the pirate chief is not far from Arthemise, she can observe this individual at will.

The man is elegant and well-armed.

On the ring finger of his left hand he wears a gold ring decorated with a black stone, slightly shiny and whose shape is irregular. His partially open shirt reveals a superb pendant hanging from his thick neck and this jewel, probably unique and also made of gold, represents a dragon, all claws out, with a gnarled body and a wide open mouth, adopting a threatening posture.

He also wears on his right wrist a beautiful gold bracelet engraved with an inscription, a mysterious word that Arthemise cannot manage to read.

The weapons attached to his belt are multiple and various: first of all a long and thin sword, whose point and blade seem to be particularly well sharpened, then a dagger inlaid with the same black stones as his ring, and at last a wonderful pistol decorated with dark and varnished wood and superbly ornamented with gilding, displaying at its extremity four barrels arranged to be flat-laid and whose original shape reminds that of a duck's foot.

However, what attracts Arthemise's most interest is the animal that stays, half-sitting half-lying, on the broad shoulder of the pirate. This strange beast might look like a cat weighing eight to ten pounds, but its thick tabby fur, featuring beautiful black stripes and dark spots on a grey and whitish background, suggests that it is a semi-wild animal. Although its ears are black-tipped and pointed, with short and black tufts, the young girl can easily recognize that it is not a lynx. Indeed, she is familiar with this kind of animal because she had often observed it from a distance when sometimes it was cautiously walking out of the great forest and moving smoothly over the snowy winter grounds. No, the beast that dozes on the man's shoulder would rather look like a kind of small panther. In fact, unlike the lynx whose tail is very short, the tail of this animal is long, bushy, covered with black circles and with a tip of the same color, which this beast shakes from time to time, probably as a sign of annoyance. Sometimes, in order to cling better to her master's garment, the little panther extends its slightly curved claws, which although thin appear pointed and sharp. As for its eyes, always half-closed, they appear as simple slits barely opening up when needed, for the sole purpose of keeping a close eye on the surroundings, and then, for a short moment, everyone can observe this cruel look with little and mysterious black pupils standing out well against a yellow-green iris.

Finally, the neck of the beast is adorned with a splendid necklace made of gilded metal, presenting a double row of sharp spikes and linked by a small chain to the pirate's belt. Arthemise carefully observes this man with a combination of surprise, admiration and fear, and then quietly speaks to her servant:

"So, Khaaly, how can this strange individual know our family name?"

"This pirate was already coming to visit us for the rum and some time ago, the former master told him your name, Mademoiselle."

"Yes, I understand, thank you Khaaly."

And now the young Viscountess finds nothing better to do than stare at this pirate. For the moment, she is not interested in the two others who accompany him but only in the supposed Captain of this little group. Undoubtedly, despite her young age, she wants to figure out what kind of man he is...

Despite his style and good manners, he is certainly not a man coming from the high society, nor is he a soldier, much less a member of the local bourgeoisie or a wealthy merchant. So, he does belong to this famous secret world of piracy, but why does he look nothing like his two mates? Inside the young mind of Arthemise, ideas are confused and chaotic... either this person is an excellent liar, a manipulator who plays with the naivety of those he meets, but who in fact is just a brute, a lout like the two others. Or perhaps there is among this tribe, a category of men who could be described as 'Pirate Lords'.

Thus, it is not only through play but also to unravel this mystery, that Arthemise, curious as always, does not stop looking intensely at this individual who is now not far from her.

Nevertheless, the pirate, wise and clever, is well aware of this interrogating glance, which is constantly questioning his person. Then, in his turn, he begins to stare at the young girl. Although they are not close to each other, they are close enough so that their eyes can defy one another and begin this calm and silent duel.

How long did this eye contact last? No one can say. Yet Arthemise was standing firm with her large and beautiful green eyes permanently focused on those darker and unfathomable of this strange man, but gradually her gaze began to get tired, from time to time she was blinking, while the pirate's eyelids were remaining permanently motionless. He was in the process of winning this confrontation and that seemed to distract and amuse him. His sinister eyes, with an indefinable color, sometimes severe, contemptuous, and sometimes mocking, ended up defeating the young girl. At last she looked down and turned to the fountain. Then the pirate added:

"What beautiful eyes, Mademoiselle De Lomvast! Two emeralds! Really magnificent!"

Arthemise doesn't say any word, she is just a little offended. Nevertheless, she does appreciate the compliment. The girl simply begins to understand that on this island, in these places, until then unknown to her, and in the company of all these new persons, she would have many things to discover and also to accept as they would present themselves.

She more or less painfully experienced this terrifying episode in the company of this spider monster and has now learned at her own expense that no one can face a 'Pirate Lord' with impunity.

Little by little, in this new life, Arthemise realizes that she is no longer entirely Mademoiselle la Vicomtesse de Lomvast, the young girl who does take everything for granted, and in front of whom family and relatives used to remain in perpetual admiration. Nonchalantly she meditates on all this by putting her pale hand in the small pond and playing with the fresh and pure water of this pleasant fountain...

Khaaly has already finished her work, and as nothing can ever escape her attention, she notices that the Viscount and the Viscountess, are on their way back to the house. She rushes immediately in order to meet her masters and warn them of the presence of these new visitors.

"Sir, Madam, the pirates have just come to our place, they're now waiting at the Grand Case."

"Thank you Khaaly, I knew that one day or another they would land here. We'll find out presently what these people want from us!"

As soon as they arrive near the fountain, the couple is politely greeted by the pirate who, for the occasion, does not fail to bow slightly as a sign of respect.

"Madame la Vicomtesse, Monsieur le Vicomte." he hastens to say with his deep and smooth voice.

"Sir." is content to answer the Viscountess, who immediately keeps walking with a surprised and upset attitude.

Madame De Lomvast enjoins her daughter and Khaaly to accompany her inside the house. Arthemise would have preferred to stay here and listen to the conversation that is being prepared between the two men, but she must resign herself to following her mother and it is therefore with her head down and a grumpy face that she moves away from the fountain and the pirate's company. Monsieur De Lomvast, for his part, begins to stand close to this strange visitor in order to observe him better and exclaims:

"Sir? Who am I speaking to?"

However, the Viscount, as he is approaching, does not pay attention that the small panther, which was dozing on the pirate's shoulder, has slightly opened her eyes and is slowly sitting up straight, because precisely she noticed the arrival of an unknown person. Then it all happens very fast. The animal, probably surprised by this sudden presence, first moves back its head a bit, in order to examine this newcomer, and rapidly opens its mouth wide and begins to howl and hiss in a particularly aggressive way towards the Viscount, while its pupils are becoming dilated with anger. Undoubtedly the pirate, well acquainted with his beast, expected such an attack and quickly hastens to hold it firmly and then tries to calm it down, in order to protect Monsieur De Lomvast:

"Shhh, guapa, queda tranquila!"

"I apologize, Monsieur le Vicomte, this small panther is half-wild and it doesn't appreciate at all the company of someone it has never met before. But please, forgive me, I didn't introduce myself. In those areas people call me 'The Dragon' and you will understand why very soon! I have been visiting this island for some time now and I was familiar with your predecessor. Thanks to this rich and fertile soil, this benevolent climate and these wonderful sugar cane plantations, he was selling me some rum, which is one of the best in the West Indies!"

Just like his daughter a little earlier, the Viscount is, to say the least, disconcerted and doubtful about this unexpected individual, for if he is elegant and polite, if his voice is harmonious and pleasant, he is nonetheless powerfully armed and the two men who accompany him have a truly awful appearance and display an unattractive look. Moreover, the presence of this wild animal resting on his shoulder makes this encounter quite unpleasant because the latter seems rather uncommon and also particularly aggressive.

However, Monsieur De Lomvast is not a man who can be easily impressed. Indeed, during his many expeditions within the Royal Navy, often accompanied by battles, he dealt with a lot worse, and then this new existence as a sugar cane farmer has consolidated his experience within this very special island environment. Thus, he manages to regain his imposing presence and finally decides to answer:

"Sir, I don't know exactly in what kind of business the former owner of the place was involved and I have nothing to do with his past activities and practices. You should know Sir, that first of all I must ensure a certain production of sugar. This was made compulsory for me when this concession was granted. As for the beverage that you seem to appreciate so much, I certainly produce some, but in small quantities, which I put in the good hands of the Franciscan monks living in this settlement."

But Monsieur De Lomvast is a wise man. He knows very well that in these remote and isolated islands pirates can very fast prove to be dangerous, then in order not to offend his visitor, he continues in a more moderate tone:

"Nevertheless, in order to please you, I can get you some rum made from molasses, as you know, this is the residues of my sugar production."

The pirate says nothing. He is just looking at the Viscount quietly and coldly, but his gaze nevertheless shows a certain amusement tinged with some mischief. Finally, after a moment that may have seemed rather long, he decides to answer:

"And you are absolutely right, Monsieur le Vicomte. Of course you owe it to yourself to honor your sugar production. However, you should know that the Tafia, this common molasses rum that you are offering me, is good only for all these British boors. My buyers are much more demanding and can't be satisfied with such a beverage! Rum, the real rum as we like it, directly made from this sugar cane juice that we used to call 'Vesou', is the finest, the tastiest and surely the most stylish drink ever made! If by any chance you would agree to produce some, of course not in large quantities but just at the expense of a few bushels of sugar, do not forget to let me know. I sail in the vicinity from time to time and some will quickly know how to warn me!"

The pirate makes a pause and smiles, as if despite the reluctance of his interlocutor, he would finally emerge victorious from this meeting:

"At last, dear Sir, you should know that I always pay for my orders in good Pieces of Eight... I hope to see you again Monsieur le Vicomte!"

The pirate bows again to greet Monsieur De Lomvast politely, then he briefly waves to his two men, who immediately follow him to the back of the Grand Case and to the steep path leading to the cove.

The three pirates have just gone in silence, as quietly and as fast as when they first arrived. It even makes you wonder if they really came thus far, or if all this was just a mere dream.

Just like the young Arthemise when she was looking at this man, the Viscount can hardly believe his eyes or his ears. The ships on which he used to sail were always heavily armed and unlikely to be attacked by pirates, who by the way had very little interest in these heavy tonnage vessels, whose cargo generally consisted solely of armed soldiers. Monsieur De Lomvast had therefore never, directly or indirectly, approached the pirates, because moreover they did not venture to visit the same ports as the royal navies.

This encounter suddenly revealed a singular and disturbing world that was unknown to him until then, a strange, indefinable and above all mysterious world, but also a world populated by people who depend on no one and seem to enjoy great freedom, an environment whose aggressiveness is hidden and which suddenly can prove to be dangerous and cruel, a faithless and lawless world without any mercy or compassion. The Viscount read all this well in the pirate's eyes and he immediately understood that this falsely soft and suave voice was actually hiding the greatest determination and inflexibility...

During the first year, the farm worked properly. Sugar production was going well and the question of producing large quantities of rum did not even arise. The molasses thus obtained were sufficient to prepare the fair quantity of Rum necessary to the priory, so that, thanks to the careful attention of the monks, it could age quietly and become better in the darkness and relative freshness of their cellar. The pirates did not show themselves anymore and if they were still living in this world, no doubt they were carrying out their trade in other islands and on other shores. But then came a day when the climate of animosity that the Viscount had created, more or less in spite of himself, because of his merciful attitude towards slaves, finally revealed itself. Lots of settlers, much more affluent than Monsieur De Lomvast, managed to organize a joint and significant sugar price reduction. The production ensured by the Viscount's farm was at risk of not being sold any longer because much too expensive, and this one had to resign himself to lower his prices in order to be in line with those practiced by his rivals. However, since the Viscount was not enjoying the same prerogatives or the same wealth as the other owners, he soon realized that time would not play in his favor, and if he kept doing so, he would not be able to meet his obligations and would be ruined in the near future. Sooner or later he would probably have to sell his farm at a very moderate price and then become forced to leave this land.

That is when the Viscount remembered the pirate's visit and recalled the tempting proposal the latter had made: 'You should know that I always pay for my orders in good Pieces of Eight'

"Pieces of Eight and in great numbers... that would be enough to bail out my finances." said to himself Monsieur De Lomvast.

"It would be good enough for me to reduce my sugar production significantly for a while, and to engage in the distillation of cane juice in order to prepare this renowned Rum made from Vesou..."

And from that day on, the Viscount devoted himself to this new activity. The farm buildings he had bought at the time of his concession acquisition were already equipped with stills that could properly ensure such a production. Moreover, the former owner had not failed to make use of them in order to manufacture this nectar, which gradually was becoming more and more famous and appreciated.

Monsieur De Lomvast managed that the pirate named the Dragon, who had once visited him, became aware of it, and some time later he was able to start selling his production to this man. Faithful to his promises, the pirate paid well and as announced with Pieces of Eight. He was perfectly satisfied with this Rum, whose strength was intoxicating and the color crystalline. Thus, this small business enabled the Viscount, of course not to get wealthier, but at least to refund his debts and to succeed in surviving.

Eventually the two men became friends, and although this agreement was mainly based on commercial interests and on a kind of professional courtesy, a great collusion and a mutual understanding developed between the two partners.

From then on the pirate was coming to the Grand Case without any escort, but of course armed as he was and still wearing his wild animal on his shoulder, he had little to fear and could have even fought a small group of individuals on his own.

Madame De Lomvast and Arthemise had long understood that this strange visitor had no intention of ill-treating their family, indeed it was quite the contrary, because Rum trade was their common business.

Some days, when the pirate was coming to anchor his ship at the entrance to the cove located in the south of the island, and while in the evening the hubbub of the exploitation had finally ceased, the two men enjoyed meeting under the gallery of the house, and comfortably seated, they were initiating various conversations which sometimes dragged on very late into the night.

Sometimes, Arthemise, who had now reached the age of thirteen, was allowed to stay with them for a while. However, the young girl was just listening to them, without ever taking part in the dialogue.

Nevertheless, that evening, the words of the two men had gradually become serious and disturbing, to say the least. To the Viscount, who was wondering how to age part of his Rum in order to give it this beautiful amber color and thus make it tastier, and finally sell it at a better price, the pirate replied in this way:

"Monsieur De Lomvast, what you are planning to do is a long and delicate operation that would require a lot of care and attention. Moreover, to get what you want, you would have to find a suitable place, sufficiently fresh and, above all, scrupulously kept secret. Is there such a place inside your property? I doubt it! It is true that the Rum you are selling me is a white and unaged alcoholic beverage, whose taste and perfume are those of a recently distilled drink, a raw product with a lot of strength but little flavor. However, this way you do not need to keep this highly sought-after beverage during a long time and so you reduce the risk of having it stolen! You can believe me, Monsieur le Vicomte, it's much better to proceed as usual, because it ensures you a steady and regular income! Didn't I always pay you in good time?"

"Of course yes Sir, certainly! You're probably right. Thanks to our small business my financial situation has improved a lot, so let's keep it that way!"

"And please don't be afraid, Monsieur De Lomvast, from time to time I will gladly provide you with this Rum of beautiful amber color and inimitable taste, so you will be able to enjoy it at your leisure! But right now you were casually talking about our various agreements and I would like you to remain on your guard..."

"Should I stay on my guard? And for what purpose, sir?"

"It's very easy to understand, your neighborhood doesn't appreciate you! The irritation, jealousy and bitterness of other settlers is great and they will never forgive you for daring to change the black code within your own farm. With all due respect, Monsieur le Vicomte, what a disastrous idea you had had that day!"

"This is my own business! Ah, your words remind me of the captain's who brought me here, the Commander of 'Le Havre de Grâce'. Come on, sir, why are you so worried? Very Soon I'll be wealthier than any of my stupid neighbors and one day I'll even be able to buy back their properties! Indeed, your idea to produce Rum instead of sugar has been absolutely wonderful!"

"Well, Monsieur le Vicomte, since you tell me that your finances are in pretty good shape at the moment, you should therefore temporarily reduce the production of Rum and resume sugar production. This option would have the advantage of appeasing all those people who observe you, and would help a little bit to make you forget..."

"And to find myself on the verge of bankruptcy again? Thank you very much, there is no question of it! But perhaps, Sir, you are no longer able to sell the merchandise that I produce... never mind, I'll put it up for sale to the native Indians!"

"That is not the problem, Monsieur De Lomvast, the filibusters I visit never have enough of this beverage! However, I have heard what is being said around here and I know that you and your family are more or less in danger. If I may insist, get back to producing only sugar and be careful not to interfere in this black code again. As for Indians, avoid trading with these people, it will just get you into trouble!"

"Can't you protect me, Sir? What is the point of being friend and accomplice of a pirate, moreover nicknamed the Dragon, if this one is unable to provide protection and support? Accompanied by your crew of louts and brutes, aren't you strong or brave enough?"

"We are, Monsieur De Lomvast, of course we are! Unfortunately, some battles are superfluous and useless! In addition, as you know, we only come to anchor in the vicinity of this island a few days a month and during our absence the worst events may happen. So, Monsieur le Vicomte, please follow my recommendations and everything will be all right! Don't worry, we will resume our business later, when your neighbors have calmed down a little..."

The punishment

But the Viscount, particularly self-confident, did not follow the pirate's advice, and as if nothing had happened, carried on with his production of Rum. Recklessly, he also persevered in the application of his new black code.

The Piasters he was collecting were gradually coming to fill his precious small box, whose location in the Grand Case was kept secret. Even his own wife, Madame De Lomvast, would not have been able to find it. As for the pirate, he kept buying the Rum but stopped advising the Viscount because he was feeling that it was no longer of any use, given that Monsieur De Lomvast still held his own ideas above all advices.

A second year has passed and Arthemise, since then a very beautiful young girl with long red hair, is now fourteen years old. She impresses people with her bearing, her slender body and her height, almost equivalent to that of her father, and in this way she is always admired by her parents and her servant Khaaly. As for her eyes, even more sparkling and pure, they still display this amazing emerald green color.

From now on, the young Viscountess has been able to acquire a certain independence and she no longer hesitates to wander alone, especially when Khaaly is too busy. Thus, some evenings, when the heavy rains have finally stopped and the sky is becoming quiet and clear, she sometimes likes to walk down the winding path to that mysterious cove that attracts her so much.

However, this night, the atmosphere is quite dry because the thunderstorms did not break out on the property but much farther away. Everything is particularly dark because at this time of the month the sky is moonless.

Arthemise has left the Grand Case very late and without making any noise. Her parents, no doubt tired, are already sleeping deeply, and the servant who, at the Viscountess's request, must from time to time spend the night in her masters' house, is surely also asleep. The girl snuck out of her room, went down the wooden stairs without making any noise, and then left through the lower window, opening directly out from the back of the main room, so she didn't have to maneuver the front door, which often tends to squeak and make an unwanted noise. At present she moves forward step by step, carefully, along the small path leading directly to the cove. Faithful to her habits and in order to remain unnoticed, she does not use any burning torch because she knows perfectly well that after some time her eyes will have become accustomed to the darkness. Yet that evening, when she finally reaches the shore, she has a lot of difficulty to make out the surface of the water because the ocean is as calm as a lake. Indeed, without any breath of air there is no foam visible on the sea. Moreover, not any sparkle nor light comes to shimmer over this nearby maritime area, thus possibly accentuating the ambient darkness. So the young girl just moves slowly along the narrow beach, but suddenly her legs stumble over something rather big and hard and that makes her jump.

"How far did I walk? Is it a tree trunk, a rock? She wonders...

She then carefully feels the unknown object and shivers again, realizing that she is touching with her fingertips a longboat beached on the sand.

The pirates! It can only be these people, because they are the only ones who know this cove and sometimes come here. They must be there, probably very close to her, but she cannot see them nor their vessel, who must be anchored at the entrance of the small bay. Maybe they have heard her arriving and they remain silent, lurking in this persistent darkness, and they watch her without saying any word, as if she had suddenly become a prey. Arthemise knows very well that if their Captain, the one called the Dragon, is part of the group, then she is absolutely safe. But what would happen if that man who commands them and has got all the power wasn't there and if on site there were only these wild, lawless and sinister individuals? The girl finally understands why her servant Khaaly never wanted to come here, and not even when the day was clear, so what madness to visit to this deserted place during the night! Arthemise calmly and as discreetly as possible begins to retreat. She does not dare to speak and ask if the Captain is there, but anyway, if this man was present, he would surely have already greeted her and offered to take her back to the Grand Case. Nevertheless, blindly, the young girl finally finds the lower part of the path and prepares to go up slowly, without making any noise and while promising herself to come down here never again.

That is when she suddenly notices a flickering light, but quite bright, and despite the distance she can smell a strong odor of burned wood.

"What is going on up there?" She says to herself... "That cannot be true! Is the Grand Case on fire?"

Then Arthemise shudders and suddenly becomes terrified because right now she remembers the pirate's words: 'However, I have heard what is being said around here and I know that you and your family are more or less in danger. If I may insist, get back to producing only sugar and be careful not to interfere in this black code again.'

Her father, the well named Viscount, never took into account the wise recommendations of this man, nor even the friendly advices of the Captain of the Frigate 'Le Havre De Grâce', and even less the repeated warnings of the intendant of the exploitation.

"Since our arrival in this colony my father has only managed to make enemies. He modified the black code, he produced much more Rum than sugar, he acted only according to his will and did nothing in accordance with the customs and traditions prevailing in the West Indies!" Whispers the young girl, who goes up this bad path as fast as she can. She often stumbles, gets up again and immediately resumes her frantic run. She lets herself be guided by the violent light of the now raging fire. Arthemise breathes fast and deeply, but then she ends up running out of breath. She tries to shout, to call her parents and Khaaly but no sound can come out of her mouth.

Suddenly a short whistle is being heard, apparently coming from the shore, and at that moment she realizes that she is followed by several men walking up the path at high speed and using flaming torches to light their way. It will probably not be long before they catch her up.

"Mademoiselle De Lomvast?"

The girl stops and turns around because she has just recognized the voice of the pirate Captain. She feels reassured and worried at the same time. So, this man was not far from the beach but why didn't he come forward sooner?

"What's happening at your home, Mademoiselle? Are your parents still in the Grand Case? Ah, I knew all this would end badly! Monsieur le Vicomte never wanted to listen to my advices!"

Arthemise cannot even get a word in because the pirate has already caught her by the arm and drags her away with his crew to the top of the hill, but when the small group finally reaches the house, it is only to discover a huge blaze and hear muffled shouts, similar to those made by Indians and which seem to come from the nearby savannah.

"Run after these individuals and bring them back to me, we're waiting for you here!" Yells the pirate at his small troop.

Immediately, following the Colossus with the red crest of hair who had already come here the first time, the men rush towards the dark vegetation, while Arthemise remains in the company of the pirate, her eyes fixed on the Grand Case, of which very soon only ashes will remain. And they both stand there, silent and motionless, helplessly watching this scene of desolation.

Suddenly time has stopped, and these two completely opposite human beings appear united in the face of a common and terrible ordeal by sharing the same consternation...

Much later in the night, the Dragon's men are coming back, stunned and upset. The Colossus shakes his head as a sign of dissatisfaction, and then he speaks to his captain:

"Nichts, Mein Herr! Not found, niemand ist hier! Not any soul around, nobody!"

"So, Let's go, we have nothing more to do here! Come with us Mademoiselle, it's already too late. It is not for lack of having warned your father but he never listened to me. As you can see, his enemies have finally took revenge!"

Usually Arthemise had most often been seen as a cold and indifferent young person, but that night the events occurred with such a speed that she cannot help but show her anger to the pirate:

"Our house has burned down! My parents and my servant are dead, do you understand? I'd rather burn myself up with them! You were there Sir and you stayed in the darkness near your longboat. You didn't even deign to come and talk to me. You could have intervened and prevented all this! And now instead of staying here you could hunt these Indians down with your crew, their villages are easy to find; you could avenge us!"

"No Mademoiselle, I'm not sure that the voices and shouts we have heard were coming from Indians, and a little earlier with my men we were getting some water at the spring located on the other side of the cove... we didn't see you. We couldn't even know you were down here. It was only by rushing towards the Grand Case that we spotted you and caught up with you."

"Did you say you were taking water at the source? On such a dark night?"

"Yes Mademoiselle, from time to time I ask my men to carry out some works in tough conditions, so that they can cope in all circumstances."

But Arthemise does not listen because her disappointment is boundless and her fury excessive.

"Ah you know how to impress people around you by wearing your kind of panther on your shoulder and always accompanied by your German barbarian holding his axe as one holds a trophy! And then what? Nobody and nothing! My parents used to like you, they trusted you, on the contrary you made fun of us and at last you abandoned us!"

She then desperately strikes the pirate's chest before bursting into tears and collapsing at his feet, exhausted and defeated...

The Dragon remains motionless and looks sadly at the young girl before bending down and taking her pale hands in his own.

"You are right, if at least my 'Guapa' had been with me, she would surely have caught up with these people. But you're wrong, we're not cowards. Mademoiselle De Lomvast, I promised your father to protect you and always meet your needs in case both your parents disappear. But right now we must leave. Those who set fire to the Grand Case mustn't know that you are still alive, otherwise they will try to find you and then kill you, for obviously you are the sole heiress of your parents. And now, precisely, you are the one and only Viscountess of Lomvast, Mademoiselle!"

The girl has somewhat calmed down, she does not say any word but she has raised her head in the direction of the pirate who is going on with his speech:

"So, follow us, let's get aboard my ship and set sail. We will leave this island, but sooner or later we will return and discover the truth. You can believe me, for these unknown people, for these cowardly and masked aggressors we will become the worst nightmare!"

The pirate captain helps Arthemise up and gives a brief signal to his men in order to get them down to the shore and prepare the longboat.

A bit later, they all embark and then the pirates begin to row vigorously to the Sloop who is anchored at the entrance of the cove.

During all this time and the times that followed, the young girl kept her head down as a sign of despair and resentment. The muscles of her face were contracted with rage, she was always clenching her teeth and not any word could ever come out of her mouth.

She so used to enjoy staring at those around her, but from now on she no longer looked at anyone. Her intense yet always pleasant and attractive gaze had suddenly become fixed in an expression of anger and disgust.

It only took a few moments for Arthemise to definitively join adulthood and leave for ever this happy and carefree youth, of which only confused and disordered memories are remaining in her thoughts...

Fierce

The Brigantine sighs strongly, and again she talks to herself, sneering:

"You scoundrels, you ended up paying for my parents' murder! A few years later we came back, with the Dragon and all his crew. We slaughtered you all, you cowards, your intendants and your henchmen! Only women, children, and slaves remained unharmed... And then we set a great fire to your properties and possessions and we left nothing but ashes! What you had patiently built and even your plantations, we destroyed everything! Only ruins were remaining! This place became cursed forever. From now on, no one will dare to venture around here. But as for me, bunch of rascals, if I had been alone I would have gladly made the pleasure last much longer. I would have killed you slowly, very slowly. Your sufferings would have been endless... "

The Brigantine remains there, listless, eyes on fire and evil memories in her mind.

"And all this happened because of a miserable edict dating from the last century, that fateful black code, and also a few barrels of rum!"

She sways back and forth, nervously, in her antique rocking chair.

But up there on deck it seems that a certain turmoil has suddenly given way to the silence and drowsiness that have prevailed since the beginning of this day, and following this moment of agitation, the Boatswain's heavy footstep can be heard in the wooden staircase that leads down to the Captain's cabin. Once in front of the door, which remained wide open, the strong man lowers his head in order to look inside the room.

"Madam?"

"Yes Colossus, what's going on?"

"Schooner in sight, off the starboard bow, half a league."

"Just one ship?"

"Yes, madam."

"How many cannons?"

"Four portholes still closed, Madam, and no cannon ready to fire."

"All right, hunt her down, then tear her sails up and break her masts, then you will order the boarding."

"At your command, madam!"

"Wait, you'll let me fight the Captain and his first Officer. I still need to have a little fun."

"Good, Madam!"

The Colossus, with his reddish crest of hair, nods and turns around. He will give his orders to the crew and very soon all those men, who were dozing, will be able to resume their favorite activity filled with battles and lootings.

The Brigantine squeezes out a smile, then she gets up and quietly moves towards the two bodies sideboard made of chiseled mahogany wood. She takes out a superbly engraved stemmed glass and pours herself a good shot of Rum. While watching the outside through one of the large portholes of her cabin, she then sips her favorite drink very slowly.

"Another old tub, we have to be prepared to accept our achievements in small doses! But it doesn't matter, a little exercise won't hurt us, and what a pleasure to terrify all those fools!"

Quietly, the young woman begins to prepare herself...

"Now let's see, what do I need? If the Captain is in the same state as his ship, my dagger will be more than enough... without forgetting my black cape and my beautiful hairy beast. Well clung to my shoulder, it always creates a sensation!"

On the deck of the vessel the men are busy and the Brigantine always likes to hear the sound of their scurrying footsteps, as well as their loud and incessant shouts, when suddenly several violent detonations are heard and come to shake the ship and pierce through the sky.

"All right, cannoneers, I already know your chained cannonballs are going to do wonders!"

One last time, the Brigantine looks at herself in her large glazing bead mirror, adorned with gilded and carefully carved woodwork.

"All dressed in black, with my long red hair covering my shoulders and my beast accompanying me, I am not too bad for impressing my next victims. Come on, it's time to get on the quarterdeck to watch the boarding and meet the Officers of that miserable schooner."

The Brigantine's men are strong, seasoned, fast and properly armed. In a deafening din they are quickly leaping on those poor, frightened and helpless sailors who do not even have the courage to escape by jumping overboard. Without any mercy they undertake to tear them to pieces and finally to slaughter them.

Firmly camped on her rear castle, the Brigantine seems to enjoy this atrocious and bloody spectacle. Finally, the smile is back on her face and her large emerald-green eyes once again display this strange expression of contentment mixed with malevolence. Everything seems almost finished and the pirates, according to the orders they have received from their Boatswain, surround the Captain and his First Officer, and then are waiting in silence, gathered on the quarterdeck of the ship they have just boarded.

Without hurrying and in order to meet these two Officers, the last two men still alive on this schooner, the Brigantine, with her careless behavior and nonchalant footstep, crosses the plank that connects the two ships. At last she moves inside the circle formed by her crew and in the direction of the one who seems to command this miserable ship. But as soon as the latter catches sight of the young woman, this Captain, already red with anger, rushes towards her, raising his sword and preparing to strike.

"Ah, so you're the one everyone's talking about! You slut!"

However, with a sharp movement, the Brigantine positions herself on her side to avoid the blow that the man tries to give her, and then she extends her long leg while suddenly pushing the back of her aggressor who stumbles, and carried away by his run-up, finishes his movement by falling heavily onto the floor. Without waiting, the young woman takes the opportunity to give him a violent thrust on the lower back with the hard heel of her boot, and very swiftly she kneels on his back, while grabbing the sword out of his hand and holding his wrist firmly to the ground. The unhappy one does not even have the time or the possibility to get up again because he is now lying on his belly and tightly immobilized. He barely manages to turn his head slightly. The Brigantine has just disabled her opponent on the quarterdeck and in order to prevent any further attack, she observes the First Officer with a sardonic eye. And then she quickly pulls her dagger out of her belt and addresses the Captain:

"A slut did you say, Sir? What an ugly word! Farewell, Sir!"

Then, slowly, but with a will that seems unwavering, the young woman puts the sharp blade of her dagger on the neck of the man who is struggling desperately, and without any pity or hesitation she slits his throat. The blood of an intense red instantly spurts from the wound on the floorboards and for a short moment the body of this poor Captain begins to shake in a frenetic and disordered way. Eventually, the Brigantine, who during all this time has not stopped looking maliciously at the first Officer, grabs her big spider still clinging to her shoulder and puts it quietly on the gaping wound of her unfortunate victim.

"Come on, my beautiful redhead, at last you may satisfy yourself. Enjoy his flesh and his blood!"

Without delay, the hideous beast, with the help of its fangs and mandibles, tirelessly and greedily begins to knead the wide open throat of the persecuted victim. No one can know if the Captain is still aware of what is happening to him. Although from time to time the man is still shaken by a few spasms, he seems to be dying, and finally his bruised body ends up being paralyzed and stiffened in an everlasting remission.

The assembled crew is witnessing this atrocious scene without saying a word and without showing any emotion, because no doubt all these hardened men have already witnessed several times this kind of abuse and many others committed by the one who commands them. Without waiting, the young woman gets up quickly and heads towards the First Officer who stares at her with a dumbfounded look.

"Well Sir, why didn't you help your Commander?" You see, when I was still the first Officer on that ship, I would have sacrificed my own life to save my Captain's!"

"How easy it is to prance around when your entire crew is protecting you!"

"Did you say 'prance around' Sir?"

The Brigantine comes so close to the Officer that their noses almost touch each other, and the man thus trapped can hardly move because he was already leaning against the ship's rail.

"You should learn Sir that during any single combat my crew always receive the order not to intervene, without regard for my life. Besides, my own life, I lost it a long time ago..."

At this precise moment the young woman remains silent, staring into space, and suddenly seems in the grip of painful memories, but very quickly she recovers and continues her tirade:

"Thus, anyone who would dare to interfere would be severely punished, even executed! So, sir, what's your decision? Do you choose to fight a duel against me, or to be killed and then die, like all those cowards who are part of your crew?"

The man appears totally disturbed, he then drops his sword and lowers his head...

"What's the point of fighting, do whatever you want!"

For a short moment the young woman says nothing, then she finally resumes her speech:

"Well Sir, you've just made the right decision, because that way you will save your life! You will know that during my boardings, I always leave one survivor, but just one. Usually it is the Captain but the latter, you will agree with me, was much too rude and stupid. You're lucky because this time you'll be this only one left! I will land you later, wherever I want, and so you will be able to report everything you have witnessed. But tell me again, Sir, what's the name of your ship?

"This schooner is called the 'Baguenaude'.

"Then you can believe me Sir, your 'Baguenaude', which means 'the one who sails around', will never sail again!"

After having wiped her bloody dagger on the First Officer's shoulder, the Brigantine turns around and addresses her crew:

"Put this one down to the hold until further notice!"

However, suddenly, from her elevated position on the quarterdeck, the young woman notices something that attracts her curiosity. At the other end of the deck, not far from the bow of that ship, she can see a sailor who is lying in the middle of a small pool of blood, but from what she is able to discern, this individual does not really look like an ordinary seaman...

"Who among you did fight and hurt that crewman? The one who is lying over there on the front of the ship?"

Immediately, the red-faced and one-eyed pirate, the one that everyone calls 'Midget' or 'Dwarf' advances towards the Brigantine:

"It's me Madam! He was going to strike me with his bludgeon! I managed to rip it out of his hands and knock him out!"

"Good, good! But anyway, fill a bucket with fresh water and empty it on his head. In case he is still alive, I want to question him and make sure of something..."

While the Midget complies immediately, the young woman picks up her spider from the unfortunate Captain's throat and puts it back on her shoulder.

"You've eaten enough, my beautiful hairy, and this feast has already lasted much too long!"

Nevertheless, the beast, which was undoubtedly hoping that this meal could continue a bit longer, tries to go down again along the cape of its supposed mistress, but in vain. Very quickly, the Brigantine moves away from the cadaver, and the red spider, which no longer knows exactly where to go, thus finds itself clung to the middle of the young woman's back.

"After all, stay here if you want! You'll come up later!"

A bucket of sea water has been abruptly emptied onto the injured sailor and he then slowly regains consciousness. The Brigantine keeps moving with her supple and slow gait towards this individual who intrigues her so much and now begins painfully to raise his head and look in the direction of the young woman. But the Brigantine continues to approach and is hardly believing her eyes. So, her first impression was the right one...

"Look at that! But who is this strange person?"

End of the second part

PIRATES 2.ARTHEMISE DE LOMVAST

Dear readers,

Thank you for having read this novel

Your comments, your reviews, either laudatory or unfavorable, are always welcome!

LucD.auteur@hotmail.com

Don't miss out!

Visit the website below and you can sign up to receive emails whenever Luc Dragoni publishes a new book. There's no charge and no obligation.

https://books2read.com/r/B-A-ZCGEB-PMDYC

BOOKS2READ

Connecting independent readers to independent writers.

Did you love *Pirates 2.Arthemise De Lomvast*? Then you should read *Pirates 3.The Meeting*[1] by Luc Dragoni!

The schooner on whom Blandine Veyre had embarked from the small island of Pantelleria was attacked by the Brigantine and her men.The young girl had no choice but to stay on board this Pirate ship, especially since she could not return to live in her hometown of Marseilles, which became devastated by a terrible plague epidemic.Blandine is wounded and her encounter with the Pirate Captain and her crew is full of sufferings and misunderstandings.The young lady from a good family discovers there an atrocious world which was totally unknown to her....Will she try to escape, to leave this nightmare, or will she attempt to get used to this new life?"When the pirates notice my absence, they will surely start looking for me but I don't think they will be able to reach me, and then, first of all, they won't even know which direction to follow! If

---

1. https://books2read.com/u/bw9OjO

2. https://books2read.com/u/bw9OjO

I continue at this pace without making any stop, I'll always be ahead of them, perhaps one league, and as soon as I get close to the village, I will finally be safe. They'll never dare to pursue me up to there and they'll have to turn around!"

Also by Luc Dragoni

Pirates 1. The Voyage of Blandine Veyre
Pirates 2. Arthemise De Lomvast
Pirates 3. The Meeting
Pirates 4. The Blood Sisters
Pirates ! 1 Le Voyage de Blandine Veyre
Pirates ! 2 Arthémise De Lomvast
Pirates ! 3 La Rencontre
Pirates ! 4 Soeurs de Sang